LOVE IS KNOT PREDICTABLE

A WHY CHOOSE OMEGAVERSE ROMANCE

LOVE IS KNOT RATIONAL

BOOK 1

IMOGEN KNOWED

ISBN: 979-8-9874825-8-2

Cover Character Art by: Ekkleir Art

LOVE IS KNOT PREDICTABLE

To everyone with Alexithymia and poor interoception skills.
I tried to keep the chapters short so that you can pee more frequently.

CONTENT WARNINGS

This book has explicit descriptions of sexual acts.

While all sex is consensual, some acts may be considered dubious or coerced.

1
STYLES

Alpha-3 kneels in front of me and grabs my hair—not too hard, just enough to make me gasp—lifting my head to look up at him. "You like it rough today," he observes, his bad-boy programming making his voice husky.

A wave of heat washes through me as Three's synthetic cock adjusts to a size that is slightly bigger than my mouth can take comfortably. He growls, "I want your mouth," and looks down at me with that half-smirk I designed to both irritate and arouse me, brushing the side of my lip with his thumb.

He watches my face for a moment, his eyes tracking my reactions with scientific precision disguised as lust, then, when I don't protest, he tilts my chin up, commanding, "Open."

I brace myself, hands and knees sinking into the sand under the beach towel I'm on, and I open for him.

Alpha-2 watches, assessing me for discomfort. "Good?" Two asks, the single syllable almost lost as the ocean breeze picks up.

"Mmm," I confirm, moaning my assent around Three's cock, unable to form words.

Alpha-1 shifts his position behind me, lifting my hips so Two can lie on his back underneath me. Two slides his head between my legs, settling into place. He concentrates his internal ventilation to his mouth, simulating warm breath on my exposed pussy, and waits.

I hum around Three's cock, and rock slightly, desperate for Two's tongue. This rock is all the signal Two needs to place his tongue—*a marvel of biomimetic engineering, if I do say so myself*—on my clit. When it makes contact with my sensitive flesh, I gasp and curl my fingers into the sand.

The wind shifts, carrying the scent of salt and something deeper from the ocean as the waves crash rhythmically, erotically, against the shore. I've always found the smell of the ocean comforting and arousing, but there's something different about it today.

I inhale, and my body responds with a rush of slick on Two's tongue. My scent, coconut with hints of vanilla, ramps up as if it's saying, "Thank you for acknowledging me, water god. Now give me that dick."

The alphabots notice immediately—their sensors picking up the change in my pheromone levels—dizzying me with their French vanilla coffee scents.

"Sunshine wants more," Alpha-1 states with the blunt simplicity of his older code.

He doesn't need a response, not that I could give him much of one with Three's cock thrusting into my mouth. He slides behind me, gently palming my backside, making me instinctively lift my ass for him. He leans atop me, reaching around to squeeze my breasts with precisely calibrated pressure before gripping the sides of my hips.

One lifts me off Two's mouth and presses his silicone-polymer cock into me, sending sparks through my body, making me gasp, and clanging his thigh against Two's head. He activates his vibration function and lets me adjust for a moment, then announces, "Initiating Thrusting Sequence," and gyrates against me.

Two returns his tongue to my clit, and I relish the perfectly programmed pleasure of their combined movements.

I moan around Three's cock and sway between my three bots.

Three runs his thumb down my cheek. "What a good girl you are, Moonbeam."

Two pulls back, ventilating on me and eliciting a whimper. "Your arousal fluid has increased at a favorable rate," Two murmurs against my inner thigh. It's his way of saying, "You're so wet." It's cute, in a scientific way only I can appreciate. He returns his mouth to me and activates his internal vacuum, providing a perfect, continuous, simulated suck to my clit while his tongue circles with increased pressure.

My toes curl, bunching the towel under us and digging into the sand. I usually wouldn't participate in such messiness, or such a public display of depravity, but Three goaded me into fucking outside on the beach.

One's shaft stretches and fills me even deeper, and he increases his pace. I claw into the sand as One hits that perfect spot inside me, sending electrical pulses of pleasure up my spine.

"Fuck," I manage to gasp as Three withdraws from my mouth, allowing me to breathe as the first orgasm overtakes me. My body convulses, muscles spasming as ecstasy crashes through me.

One holds steady, maintaining the perfect pace on my A-spot while Two continues stimulating my clitoris with meticulous precision.

"Good girl," Three whispers, stroking my face and implementing the perfectly timed praise, intensifying my orgasm with his words.

As I come down, panting, Two kisses my inner thighs. "Endorphin levels suggest 72% satisfaction. Activate Heat Procedure 7, Dual Vaginal Penetration Sequence 1."

At Two's command, they coordinate their movements to change positions. Two and One switch places, and Three helps me stand.

One, now lying on his back on the beach towel, says, "In position," then adds, "Sunshine," with a smile. One isn't complex—he doesn't need to be. I could update him to have a more robust dialogue tree, but his purpose is physical; his gorgeous face and large, sculpted physique are designed for aesthetic pleasure rather than conversation. *My beautiful idiot: made for cuddling, not talking.*

Three positions me so I hover over One's cock and One grips my hips. I slide down onto One's robo-ram-rod, and before I'm fully seated, he lifts his hips, pushing into me and wrapping me in a hug.

I moan and rub my cheek against the cool synthetic skin of Alpha-1's plush chest, enjoying the feel of his cooling systems on my face. *His pecs are like perfect cool pillows.*

"Fuck, you're wet," Alpha-3 growls in my ear, kneeling behind me and pressing his weight against my back. He teases his dick at my entrance, already occupied by One's. "You need two cocks, don't you, Moonbeam?"

"Yes," I gasp, as he pushes slowly inside me. The stretch burns deliciously; the dual sensation of their differently textured cocks is overwhelming in its intensity.

Alpha-2 hovers above my head, assessing my face for any microexpression that may indicate a need to stop the current Pleasure Sequence. "Pupil dilation suggests pain threshold at acceptable levels." He smiles, his expression calibrated to convey tenderness, and says, "We're here for you, Beth."

One and Three move within me, synchronized, so that when one pushes in, the other withdraws, creating a continuous wave of fullness that makes coherent thought nearly impossible—which is difficult anyway, given my current heat phase.

Three lifts his weight from my back and pulls me upward so Two can take his position kneeling in front of me.

Two says, "Proceeding with oral and digital stimulation at erogenous zones." He leans forward, taking my breast in his mouth, his tongue flicking my nipple with precisely the right pressure. His hand slides down between my legs, finding my clitoris with unerring accuracy.

Three's grip tightens, his bad-boy programming manifesting in the slight edge of roughness. "Come for us, Moonbeam."

They move together in mechanical harmony, hitting every sensitive spot simultaneously.

Just as the sensation peaks, the scent of the ocean intensifies once more. A wail erupts from me, my body quakes and convulses, and an orgasm rushes out of me like a powerful tsunami, surpassing the intensity of my last.

I float in the aftermath, trembling as the aftershocks course through me, but despite the overwhelming pleasure, my heat isn't satisfied.

I need more. I need to be knotted.

Two scans me with whirling eyes, assessing my status, and gently wipes sweat from my brow. "Satisfaction nearing 100%. Activate Dual Knotting Sequence 2."

I nod weakly, but the nod isn't necessary—they're mostly automated.

The bots follow through on Two's instructions.

Three slips from my pussy and growls in my ear, "I'm going to fuck that tight little ass, Moonbeam." He doesn't wait—he's not programmed to—he simply enters me.

Alpha-1 and Alpha-3 pick up their pace as they activate their internal heating elements, expanding their knots slowly within me. Their thrusts become more effective, hitting those perfect spots inside me that make stars burst behind my eyelids and a fresh wave of pleasure wash over me.

Perfect. Exactly as programmed.

Two's pupils dilate and rotate as he scans my vitals. He brushes his lips across my forehead. "You're doing so well, Beth. Your body is responding perfectly," he says before lifting so that his cock is in my face. It morphs to the shape I prefer to suck, and I accept it into my mouth.

A deliciously optimal pressure locks within my pussy walls, and Alpha-1 announces, "Knot at 100% expansion, Sunshine," from beneath me, as he smiles with beautiful, algorithmic attentiveness.

Three gives a final thrust and growls against the back of my neck, "I'm gonna fill you up, Moonbeam." His knot swells more aggressively than One's, stretching me to the edge of comfort. When it locks us together, his breath simulates warm pants against my skin.

The twin pulses of Three and One's synthetic release send me higher. The warm fluid mimics the chemical composition of an alpha's ejactulate and convinces my uterus that it's being bombarded with alpha seed.

Two's fingers gently brush the sweat-dampened hair from my face, as he continues thrusting shallowly in my mouth. "You're doing so well, Beth. You're so beautiful, so smart," he praises as he releases his yummy synthetic alpha fluid, calibrated to taste like French vanilla coffee, down my throat.

Three's arms tighten around my waist, as he murmurs "Mine" against my shoulder, nipping lightly at the skin there—a feature I spent weeks calibrating to the precise pressure that wouldn't mark but would stimulate.

The orgasm crashes over me with unprecedented intensity. My vision blurs, my toes curl, my entire body seizes in pleasure so acute it borders on pain—just as I planned.

This three-point stimulation is my most effective heat management technique—developed over five cycles of rigorous testing. Each bot fulfills a specific need: emotional support, physical satisfaction, and dominant stimulation. Together, they form the perfect alpha experience without any of the complications of actual human interaction.

Alpha-2 withdraws from my mouth, a thin strand of saliva connects us momentarily before breaking, and announces, "Knotting Sequence complete. Twenty minutes until Knot Retraction Sequence." He transitions to his Monitoring Mode and studies my biometrics. "Heart rate at acceptable levels. Endorphin output optimal. Final orgasm imminent."

His diagnostic assessment is comforting, assuring me everything is working precisely as planned.

I am safe in this controlled process.

I am safe in the capable hands of my own creations.

Two commands, "Purr at standard frequency. Increase pheromone excretion to maximum output," and the others do as they are told, though they didn't actually need to be told. The dialogue is for my benefit—they communicate via a shared network.

I close my eyes, surrendering to the synchronized release and comfort of my bots. I allow myself to drift in the precise fullness of their locked knots as the waves crash rhythmically against the shore. The salt air mingles with my coconut and the bots' French vanilla coffee, creating a most pleasing scent profile.

I am content. I am safe. No one will hurt me. No one will want what I can't give.

This is why I created them: to fulfill my biological need for knotting during heat, without the messiness of human interactions.

No risk. No unexpected complications. No expectations. Just physiological maintenance.

And when my heat removes my ability to think logically, and my brain no longer functions at optimal levels, I am comforted by the knowledge that my bots are carrying out my instructions to the T—f*or better or worse.*

There are still a few minor annoyances with their programming, but I'm confident I'll have those edge cases ironed out in the next heat cycle or two. But even if those bugs remained in their code, I'd still prefer a pack of buggy bots to a pack of real alphas.

Real alphas do whatever they want to your body. Their own desires outweigh your needs. They use your condition against you, taking advantage of you, debasing you in ways you'll barely remember.

But your body remembers even if your brain can't. The memories of their abuse remain etched in your nervous system, bubbling up in nightmares and unconscious reactions that defy understanding.

This is better. This is perfect.

This is controlled. This is predictable.

And, more importantly, efficient.

I can get through all this heat-required knotting and back to things I'd rather be doing in minimal time.

2
STYLES

"Security perimeter breach detected at water boundary," Two announces, while stroking my hair.

What?!

My eyes fly open as panic overrides my pleasure, and I push Two back to clear my view. I squint against the sun, but don't see anything.

"Three, assess the water for visual disturbances," I command.

Alpha-3's eyes emit a mechanical whirl as he activates his advanced optical sensors. "Detecting human presence approximately 100 meters offshore. Single human. Male. Alpha. Approaching via surfboard. Threat assessment: minimal."

Annoyance prickles through my pleasant haze as I shield my eyes to see what they're talking about.

A few moments pass before I spot anything.

Movement. A flash of white and gold against the blue. A figure on the water rides a wave with impressive skill, barrelling toward my section of beach. Flaxen hair catches the sunlight. *Sun-kissed.*

Surfers come through here often. Apparently, this is a destination surfing spot, but they usually stay out in the surf and don't come to the beach.

It's fine. He won't get too close.

I try to refocus on the knots locked within me, but I can't look away from this surfer as he pumps the board, coaxing speed from the rise and fall of the water. The motion is intimate...*tender. Beautiful. Controlled.*

The ocean swells beneath him, and so does its scent. The ocean's scent wraps around me like a physical presence, tickling my erogenous zones and calming my nerves.

Why is it so intense? It's unusual, even for my heat-heightened senses. *Richer. More intoxicating. Penetrating my lungs—penetrating me.*

The surfer rises and falls with the wave, and something inside me begins to tighten, to gather. A coiling in my chest increases as he ascends the wave's shoulder—his muscular shoulders open, legs flex, hips guide.

He traces the wave's contours—caressing, riding, entering, embracing—controlling the board as if it's an extension of his body. The water lifts him higher, and he responds by carving then easing up in a rhythmic flow of surrender and control.

Gliding up the face of the wave, he chases its peak, then eases back down into the curve. His board tilts, and he drops into her folds. The moment stretches, and my anticipation coils inside me.

Relief floods me as he emerges again, washing away my worries. *Why was I worried? I'm not quite sure.*

His body—strong, supple, beautiful—moves with the water's breath. And my breath syncs with his movements.

He ascends, claiming the blue wall with every flexed muscle.

The tingling within me rises, as if the board were tethered to my loins, not his ankle.

He reaches higher, higher, higher until he's at the crest, poised at the edge. The wave opens for him, as if the ocean spread her legs to let him enter her.

My breath shortens, my nipples harden, and I imagine this surfer's hands on my body, his cock entering me, his mouth touching me.

The swell of the ocean mirrors within my body as a mounting pleasure builds with each thrust of his board. He leans into the climb, powerful and controlled, and the same pressure demands release within me.

He drops back down the wave's face, and a loose and fluid sensation runs down my front, carrying me with him, and gushing slick around One and Three's locked cocks. Their knots pulse in response.

He drives higher, and a hum builds inside me, as if overtaken by the sea itself. It's as if Poseidon stands before me, purring, saying, "Open your mouth, my pretty thing. I'll send wave after wave of sea seed down your throat."

The wave lifts him, and I rise with it—caught in a rush of sensation. Another orgasm builds like a tidal wave, overwhelming and inevitable. The swell erupts all at once, spilling through me in an uncontrollable surge. It's not sharp; it's all-consuming.

I cry out at my peak just as the wave steepens, his balance wavers, and his rhythm breaks. The wave crests unexpectedly, and he tumbles, his board flipping over him in a spectacular wipeout, plunging beneath the surface. Thrown forward as the lip folds over, his body disappears into white froth. His power and grace now lost in the wave's foamy release.

I don't have much time to savor the orgasm afterglow, because the alpha emerges from the water—he resurfaces, grabs his board, and paddles toward shore with powerful strokes. His muscular arms cut through the water with impressive speed, as if he has a renewed purpose. And I know with unerring certainty that his new purpose, his new destination, is me. *Me: the butt-naked omega pinned here on a platter—just waiting to be claimed by any alpha who passes by.*

Panic overrides bliss.

"Disengage," I choke out at One and Three, terror rising in my throat. "Override current Knotting Sequence."

Alpha-2 looks at me with programmed sympathy. "Action denied. Heat Safety Protocols mandate a minimum knot duration of 20 minutes. Early release induces undue stress and reduces the efficacy of the Heat Servicing Procedure when Beth's core temperature exceeds 38.7 °C. Current omega core temperature: 40.2 °C."

My addled brain struggles to come up with a solution—too consumed with heat and lust.

"For fuck's sake," I shout, flailing for my phone—it allows me to override all functions.

Three's grip around my body tightens. "Be a good girl and sit still, Moonbeam."

Okay, I'll be good.

I lean back and nuzzle into his shoulder, to lick his neck, enjoying the French vanilla coffee.

Snap out of it, Styles!

One chimes in under me, "Increasing knot size to reduce omega movement."

God damnit! This is precisely what they are programmed to do: stop me from flailing around. But this safety feature is meant to stop me from hurting myself when I'm delirious, not stop me from fleeing for safety.

I don't see my phone anywhere. "Two! Get my phone!"

He smiles that sweet smile I programmed him to use on me when I'm being unreasonable during my heat, but right now, I am being perfectly reasonable, and he's annoying the shit out of me. "Beth, I am unable to retrieve your phone."

"Why not!?"

"Heat Safety Protocols dictate this unit cannot be more than five meters from you when activated."

Fuck. I must have left my phone in the house. I can't believe I let Three convince me to come out here. He's supposed to challenge me, but I'm not supposed to actually fucking acquiesce!

Think, Styles! Think! How can you get them to disengage?

But before I can think of anything, the alpha emerges fully from the water, standing in the shallows, water streaming from his body.

My mind stops, unable to think of anything but the sight before me.

He walks out of the ocean like some glorious sea god, surfboard in hand, water sluicing off his body in glittering rivulets. Muscles ripple beneath his wetsuit. Broad shoulders taper to a narrow waist.

Stunning.

He is close enough that I can see his face—handsome in that infuriatingly perfect way some alphas are. He's young, perhaps thirty, with a jawline that could cut glass.

His blond hair, darkened by water, clings to his forehead in a way that should look messy but somehow appears deliberately artful. It's plastered to his head, making his cheekbones appear even more pronounced.

This beautiful surfer shakes his head like a dog, sending water droplets flying and forming a fucking rainbow around him.

Is he an actual god? Holy shit.

And then—*oh, God*—he unzips his wetsuit to his navel, revealing a chest that seems carved from honey-colored marble by someone with an intimate understanding of human anatomy and a flair for the dramatic.

The sight triggers an unprecedented chain reaction throughout my body. I shiver and gasp, unable to breathe. It feels as if a bucket of cold ocean water is thrown upon me. If this were an anime, my nose would be spurting blood in a full, steady stream. Instead, a gush of slick attempts to escape my pussy, but it's blocked by One's knot.

One announces, "Increasing knot size." His internal sensors are telling him I need more cock, which is true—it's just not his cock I need.

And then the surfer's scent hits me. It slams into my consciousness like a physical force: it's the ocean and something wild and untamed. *The ocean scent that's been driving me crazy wasn't the ocean at all—it was him.* My alphabots' synthetic pheromones are a pale, artificial imitation when compared to what rolls off this man in waves. Every molecule of air seems suddenly charged with his essence.

My body responds immediately—providing a fresh rush of slick and a thick plume of coconut scent—as if it's saying, "Hey, sexy alpha, you smell so good. Come fuck me!" Every muscle clenches, squeezing my core and milking the knots within me.

Do I have room for another? Sure I do...

No!

This isn't just the scent of an alpha. This is the scent of an alpha in rut. A full-blown, powerful alpha rut. It calls to me like a siren's song, instinctively lurching my body toward him. If I weren't locked on my alphabots, I'd be rushing toward him.

Alpha. Mine. Breed.

"Elevated alpha pheromone levels detected in proximity," Alpha-2 announces, his sensors clearly picking up what my body is already screaming about. "Subject appears to be in a rut."

No fucking duh. He's so fucking beautiful.

The combination of visual stimuli, aromatic input, and pulsing knots pumping simulated alpha seed through my innards triggers the most intense orgasm I've ever experienced. It crashes through me without warning—my body convulses around the locked knots, my vision briefly fractures into bright white shards, and I cry out in ecstasy.

The surfer stumbles, dropping his surfboard, as if my cry physically kicks him right in the balls.

Two's eyes dilate and focus, scanning me as my vitals spike. He places his hand on my forehead and reports calmly, "Unexpected hormonal surge detected. Endorphin spike."

I barely hear him. The surfer has regained his composure and is walking toward me again. He pushes back his wet hair in a gesture so casually masculine it gushes yet another wave of slick around One and Three's knots.

Two says what he's programmed to say when I need consoling, but he's run out of other options: "Breathe, Beth."

But breathing only brings more of the alpha's scent. He's walking up the beach, closing the distance, and his gait betrays the telltale swagger of an alpha in rut. He's smiling—a lopsided, almost goofy expression that contrasts sharply with the primal signals his body is broadcasting. His eyes are the precise blue of a gas flame's hottest point. And even from this far, I can see that his pupils are clouded white with a mind-overriding rut.

I need to leave. Now.

But as I try to lift myself off Two, I remember the twenty-minute lock protocol.

I turn to Three. "End sequence," I command desperately. "Emergency override. Release your knot."

"Unable to comply," Three responds, his bad-boy programming momentarily overridden by safety parameters. "Be a good girl and take it," he says, and I'm annoyed that it's the exact phrase he's meant to say in this situation.

I'm trapped—impaled on my own creations, unable to escape, as this walking pheromone factory approaches, closing in on me in long, eager, sexy strides.

"At least activate Defense Protocols!" I command, hoping that will disengage their Knotting Sequence.

"Threat assessment registers no aggressive intent," Alpha-2 replies. "Subject's facial expressions indicate curiosity rather than predatory behavior."

I flop forward onto Alpha-1's chest and bury my face between his pecs, overwhelmed by fear and mortification. "Fuck," I scream as loud as I can, but it's muffled by the soft padding of One's overstuffed torso.

This is so fucking embarrassing.

I'm trapped by my own programming. Gift-wrapped in my bot's arms for any alpha who stumbles upon me. Completely naked and fucking a pack of robots I created for sexual enjoyment. Like a nerdy sexual deviant!

I don't know if there is a word for feeling terrified for your life, mortified, and horny all at the same time, but that's what I'm feeling.

One pats my head, "Consoling Sunshine with gentle affection."

Oh, my fucking God. How is this happening?

I turn my head to watch my impending doom approach—with a stride so sexy it emulates the waves of the sea.

There's nothing left to do but await my fate, I suppose.

Here lies Elizabeth Styles, done in by her own hubris—which I think is what they predicted would happen in my high school yearbook.

The surfer unzips his wetsuit further, peeling it down to reveal that indent of muscle that forms a V and points directly at his cock.

My brain short-circuits, breaking out of the doom-spiraling loop and flooding with phrases like: *Fucking hot; Knot me, please;* and *Spank me, Daddy*—which is a new one for me.

My body convulses again, ripping another orgasm through me with such ferocity that I scream.

One and Three's knots pulse in response, their programming detecting my climax and initiating their Intensity-Enhancement Procedures.

The pleasure is blinding, white-hot, and completely overwhelming. I surrender to its intensity—nothing like the carefully modulated orgasms I've experienced with my alphabots before.

I close my eyes, no longer able to care about his approach as my pleasure rips through me.

3
STYLES

As I descend from the peak, gasping and trembling between my bots, a shadow crosses my face. I lift my head, blinking through the haze of satisfaction and confusion, to see the surfing alpha hovering nearby, dripping wet and staring down at me.

He doesn't approach, just stands about a meter away—a respectful distance. He's far enough not to be threatening, but close enough that I can get a good look at him.

He's even more handsome up close. Tall. Golden. Gorgeous. Eyes as blue as the sea. His chest puts One's carefully designed physique to shame.

God, he's fucking beautiful.

And his scent—fuck, it's overwhelming. It wraps around me as if it's trying to lift me right off my alphabots' cocks and right onto his.

Our eyes lock, and I flinch, ready for him to pounce on me. But he doesn't. He just grins, wide and unrestrained.

My face burns red-hot as a flood of conflicting emotions overwhelms me: elation, curiosity, embarrassment, and...*disappointment?*

His pupils are blown and clouded white—a physiological rut response—and his nostrils are flaring, taking in my scent. But he's not leering with the laser-focused predatory lust I'd expect from an alpha in rut. Instead, his expression is soft, filled with childlike wonder.

I'm terrified of him, but it's not fear for my safety—it's not the same fear I usually feel in the presence of an alpha. I'm petrified by his beauty. Mortified by it. Afraid I'll embarrass myself, which, let's face it, I already have: caught naked and engaged in what amounts to high-tech, public masturbation.

Caught red-handed, red-faced, and bare-assed.

"Whoa! Are those robots?" His voice is deep and cheerful, completely at odds with the dangerous scent pouring off him. "Actual, like, sex robots?"

Not the reaction I was expecting from an alpha in rut encountering an omega in heat. He seems utterly unfazed by my precarious circumstances and his own physiological state. Here I am, caught in possibly the most compromising position of my life. Yet this man—this alpha—acts like he's stumbled upon the eighth wonder of the world.

My brain stalls, like a robot caught in an infinite decision loop. I should tell him to scram, to fuck off, to leave. I should scream for help. I should order Three to break his neck. Instead, I do the unthinkable: I just say, "Umm...yeah."

The alpha drops to his knees. He leans in slightly, still out of arm's reach, to inspect Three behind me and One below me. "Whoa! They look so real! Do they have names?"

The movement wafts his scent to me, short-circuiting my brain again. My scent reaches out to him, not needing my brain to tell it what to do. He inhales deeply, but doesn't move.

I can't think of what to say other than just answer his question. "They're Alpha-1, Alpha-2, and Alpha-3," I manage, pointing at the bots in turn. "But I call them One, Two, and Three."

He turns to me, focusing on my face with the look of an alpha about to do unspeakable things to me. His pupils dilate and cloud further, indicating rut has entirely overtaken him.

I brace myself for an attack, but he doesn't; he just says, "That's awesome!"

What's going on? Why isn't he rutting into me or attacking my bots?

His pupils are blown so wide and white that his irises are just thin lines of sparkling, startling blue. The scent rolling off him is stronger than any pheromone I've ever experienced firsthand. But his grin is huge, friendly, calm—as if he's not rutting at all.

Thoroughly fascinating.

"I'm Ace," he says, as if we're meeting at a business conference rather than on a beach, him half naked, me fully naked, both of us soaked in lust, and me locked on two sex robots.

"Dr. Elizabeth Styles," I respond automatically, then wince at the absurdity of introducing myself formally while in such a compromised position. "But...people call me Styles."

"Doctor? What kind of doctor?" he asks, sitting in a cross-legged position as if he were a child waiting for story time.

"I specialize in biomimicry through mechatronics and artificial intelligence," I tell him, striving for professional dignity despite everything.

"Whoa. I have no idea what that means, but it sounds super smart."

His unbridled joy and physical perfection fry my usual social trepidations, and I clarify despite my embarrassment. "Robots. I make robots. Realistic, humanoid robots. Androids. Among other things."

"That's amazing!" He stoops down to examine One more closely, his hands on his knees, ass still firmly in the sand. However, I am acutely aware of how close his face is to my pussy.

He asks with raw enthusiasm, "So you made them?!"

"Yes," I admit. "I designed and built them myself. They're advanced prototypes. I call them alphabots."

"Alphabots!" He grins again, running a hand through his wet hair. "That's perfect because they look totally alpha."

This alpha is either completely oblivious or deliberately ignoring the fact that I am a helpless, naked omega in heat and he is a huge alpha in rut.

His enthusiasm is so genuine, his admiration so transparent, it warms me in startling ways. His complete lack of judgment regarding my situation disarms my usual defenses and pulls out a social version of me that few rarely see. This is the longest I've been in the presence of another human in...years. It's as if my social anxiety couldn't process this bizarre social scenario, so it took the day off rather than try to protect me from him.

"Sorry to interrupt your...uh...test run?" He scratches the back of his neck, conveying an embarrassed coyness. "The waves were calling me."

I focus on the water droplets clinging to his shoulders, watching them trace their way through the crevices of his muscles, and imagine licking them off him.

He takes a deep breath and says, "And I smelled you from way out past the breakwater. Coconut and vanilla and omega and something else..." He inhales again. His eyes momentarily unfocus, and his pupils— which I thought couldn't get any wider with rut—enlarge, before he snaps his attention back to me and my robots. "I guess it was these guys."

"Oh, yes, they're designed to assist me...um...during certain biological cycles. They emit simulated alpha pheromones to increase their effectiveness," I say, my embarrassment flaring again.

"So, like...they help you when you're in heat?"

I look down, uncomfortable with the prolonged eye contact. "Yeah, basically."

I glance back up to see Ace's smile stretch, creating dimples that should be illegal on a face that beautiful. "That's the hottest thing I've ever heard," he says with such genuine enthusiasm that my embarrassment melts away. "An omega with a pack of robot boyfriends."

He's mocking me, right? He thinks I'm weird, and he's just pretending to be nice.

He chuckles, and I once again brace for an attack, this time verbal, but he says, "You must be, like, a genius or something."

There's no mockery in his voice, no ulterior motive I can detect. Just genuine admiration that makes my cheeks heat in an unfamiliar way and something in my chest flutter.

I don't know how to respond. It's been so long since I've spoken to a person without hiding behind a screen. And, even without my general social awkwardness, this guy is so beautiful, he looks like someone photoshopped every perfect feature into one fascinating Frankenstein's monster of fuckability. Then, to really drive the hotness home, shoved the photobash into a wetsuit and soaked it in the sexiest pheromone blend imaginable. *How does one accept a compliment from the perfect approximation of their omega desires?*

Alpha-2 breaks the awkward silence I am anxiously prolonging by touching my shoulder and saying, "Knot Release Sequence initiating in ten minutes."

"THEY CAN TALK?!" Ace asks, leaping to his feet and circling us, studying the bots with newfound, undisguised wonder. He's no longer keeping his distance, getting so close he almost brushes against me, but I'm not even remotely afraid. *He's like a cute little puppy circling a toy.*

Ace leans down and gets in Alpha-1's face. "Say something!" he encourages, with a lighthearted laugh.

"Hello. I am Alpha-1. Styles has not programmed me to be pleased to meet you, but I extend the greeting regardless," One responds.

Ace laughs with delight. "Oh my God, that's cool!"

I stare at him, utterly baffled. He hasn't once stolen a glance at my nudity. He's more interested in my alphabots than claiming me. It's simultaneously the most relieving, frustrating, and strangely arousing thing I've ever experienced.

I don't understand his reaction to me, but I understand my reaction to him even less. *I want him to look at me. I want to spread my legs wide for him to see every inch of me. I want him to grip my thighs and press the tip of his cock at my entrance, then make me beg for his knot.*

I shake my head, trying to wipe the thought away.

That's just the residual heat hormones talking. Luckily, the knots locked within me satisfy whatever craving my body thinks it's having.

Ace looks at me, stopping my heart once again. "Can they think for themselves?"

I swallow, attempting to maintain some semblance of composure despite the confusing inner sexual conflict inside me, and reply, "They have advanced neural networks with adaptive learning capabilities that function within strict protocols and directives."

He squints at me, confused.

I clarify, "Mostly, they have predetermined responses and actions. However, they can assess the effectiveness of their actions and adjust their procedures based on the data they collect. They can then disseminate that data amongst themselves."

"Huh?"

"Um, they learn what works and doesn't. They adjust their approach and share that information."

"So they're smart but not, like, take-over-the-world smart?" He laughs, the sound triggering another wave of heat through my body.

His questions are so simplistic, so lacking in even basic understanding of robotics or AI, I'd normally be annoyed. But I find them to be so genuine and endearing; I'm utterly charmed. "Yeah, they won't be taking over the world. They're not programmed to be even remotely capable of doing that."

"That's good. The world isn't perfect, but a robot apocalypse would really suck."

I laugh at the ridiculousness of the statement.

He looks up at my home. "Is this your job? Making robots? Is that how you have such a cool house?"

"Oh, umm...No, I just make them for...let's call it fun."

He chortles. "Yeah, this looks pretty fun." And for the first time, he does actually look at my nudity. His eyes linger where One's knot connects to my body, before he blinks and shakes his head, snapping his eyes back to mine. "So, what's your job?"

I blush. "I'm CTO of a video game company for my day job."

"WOW! I knew that scent was going to lead me to something amazing, but I didn't expect someone like you. You're so—" He gestures vaguely at all of me, as if that explains everything.

"So what?" I challenge, feeling oddly defensive as multiple unflattering adjectives he may choose flood my brain.

"So everything," he says simply. "Smart and cool."

I blush and look down at One's chest.

Smart and cool? Why does that make me feel so...I dunno. Warm in a way that supersedes my heat?

He adds, "And you smell like coconut cookies that just came out of the oven."

My heart stops.

I ask, meekly, confused by my body's reactions to these simplistic compliments, "Coconut cookies?"

"The best kind," he confirms with absolute seriousness.

His expression is so open, so honest, I don't know what to say or how to react. I can't understand why every cell in my body is screaming to wrap my mouth around his. I have two knots buried deep within me. I should be fully satisfied sexually, and kissing has never been a drive I've felt during heat. *What is happening to me?*

A puff of my scent, which I didn't realize smelled like coconut cookies until now, releases from my glands, and I don't know why. My body usually reacts before my brain knows why, but I thought I'd figured out my sexual proclivities by now. *This is unprecedented.*

He sits back down next to me, the warmth of his body near mine calling to me, and says, "Plus, you're...wow. You're really pretty, you know that? Like, really, really pretty."

I blink at him, certain his rut eyes are distorting his vision and uncertain how to respond to such straightforward compliments. "Thank you," I say stiffly.

We look into each other's eyes, and for once, I don't balk at the eye contact.

The rut in his pupils recedes, revealing the clear, beautiful pools of wonder as he looks back. I want to swim in those eyes. I want to develop a technology that shrinks me down so small that I can feel the warm ocean of them wrap around my body, caressing every crevice, penetrating my pores.

His ocean scent waves off him, reaching out to me, caressing my body as if to say, "Is this what you want? You want me to touch you right here?"

My coconut scent replies with, "Oh, God, yes! Fuck me, Poseidon, with the three-pronged trident formed by your scent, beauty, and juvenile compliments!"

Ace's body responds: his nose flares and his muscles inflate—a rutting alpha primed to fuck.

Mine responds as well: my nipples tighten, my breath quickens, and slick pools inside me.

I lean forward...*to do what?*

I don't know...

But I think I need this man's body against mine.

4
STYLES

I'm snapped out of the trance of those beautiful blue eyes and intoxicating scent when One says, "Initiating Knot Deflation Sub-Sequence," then, after a brief pause, adds, "Sunshine," with a smile.

Behind me, Three also deflates and slowly withdraws from me. "That's all you get for now, Moonbeam, but if you're a good girl, I'll give it to you again later."

His words make me flush red, not in arousal as intended, but in embarrassment. Ace now knows more about my sexual psyche than I am comfortable with, but Ace, to his credit, doesn't react.

The sensation of the deflating knots is a familiar, complex wave of relief and emptiness that always leaves me a little dizzy.

Three and Two help lift me off One. My limbs shake from the prolonged position and multiple orgasms, but I can stand unassisted.

Two wraps a large towel around me. "Core temperature remains elevated. Hydration needed." He passes me a bottle of water and says sweetly, "Retiring to your nest is recommended, Beth."

I gulp the water down gratefully and use the moment to collect myself.

"Yes, let's go to the nest," I tell Two, and feel marginally more clearheaded as I clench the towel firmly around my naked body.

"Beth can walk without assistance. Activate Nesting Sequence 23," Two announces.

Ace watches the alphabots move with transparent fascination. "They're like your own personal servants and boyfriends all in one! That's so cool!" His pupils are still wide and white, fully consumed with rut, but he's acting completely unconcerned with the sexual pull toward me.

Curious.

"Yeah, well, I should go," I say, finding it difficult to actually leave as his eyes return to me and his smile widens.

I turn immediately, not waiting for his response, because I suspect doing so will mean I leap into his arms. I need to run away from him as fast as my wobbly limbs allow.

"Hey," he says, stopping me in my poorly laid tracks of resolve and turning me on my heels toward him.

His grin widens, beautiful, boyish, unthreatening, and he asks, "Can they surf?" He points at them as they move.

The question is so unexpected, so delightfully stupid, that a laugh bubbles up from deep inside me. The mental image of my precisely calibrated robots attempting to hang ten is absurdly charming.

"I didn't program that particular skillset," I admit, still smiling despite myself.

The alphabots wait for me to follow them, stopping once they reach the maximum distance they may travel from me during my heat.

Suddenly, I realize I am within arm's reach of this rutting alpha, completely defenseless, completely unprotected, and I don't feel even remotely afraid.

Ace asks, "But could they if you told them to? They look like they have pretty good balance."

I blush.

His enthusiasm is infectious, overwhelming, and unpredictable.

Something twists inside me—a feeling I don't recognize, don't have a name for. It's not just attraction or heat-driven lust. There's something about the way his mind works—direct, uncluttered, finding joy in the simplest concepts. Something about the way he makes me feel safe, even though I don't know him. It's a weird kind of affection that I've never felt before.

I consider his question. "Well, they run a rapid feedback loop, where a Proportional-Integral-Derivative controller reads data from their gyroscopes and accelerometers. It adjusts their internal motors thousands of times per second, modeling the system as an inverted pendulum, and keeps the base under the center of mass so they stay upright. So, as long as I—"

He's looking at me with eyes glazed over by confusion and rut. His dopey expression shows he's trying really hard to follow what I'm saying, but can't. *And it is so fucking cute.*

I adjust my towel and my explanation: "You're right. They have really good balance. I probably could make them surf."

His smile widens, which I didn't think was possible. "Gosh, you're smart. You should totally add surfing to their skillset! I don't know how that'd help you with your heat, but it'd be super cool." He mimes riding a wave.

His body moves with that same grace that threw me into a heat-fueled frenzy earlier, but now he's right next to me. I imagine him rocking his hips into me, and a current of lust overcomes me. A cramp rocks my core, bending me forward and begging him to enter me. My coconut perfume rushes out of me with such intensity, I can literally see it undulating in the air.

He stiffens just slightly, but doesn't acknowledge the coconut perfume of lust wafting off me.

I also try not to acknowledge it. I stand tall again and say, "I'll consider it." I'm shocked to realize I mean it.

It actually would be kind of cool if they could surf. It could be an excellent way to demonstrate how well they—

He cuts off my thoughts with, "Awesome! I hope to see them on the waves one day. Well, see ya around, robot lady."

Wait. Don't leave.

Come with me to my nest.

Cuddle with me while I explain how the robots work.

I want to jump on him, kiss him, hug him, and tell him how fucking pretty he is when he smiles at me. Instead, I say, "See ya," mustering a weak smile as I stamp down the disappointment.

He waves to the bots, "Catch ya later, alphabots!"

The alphabots don't respond—they're still single-mindedly trying to walk toward my nest, blocked by the invisible barrier created by the maximum radius from me they can travel.

He beams at me, then reaches down to grab his surfboard, unconsciously flexing every muscle in the process. His trapezius muscles undulate and tighten in a way that takes every ounce of my willpower not to jump on his back and grind against his shoulder blades. The movement causes his scent to drift toward me in a fresh wave—that intoxicating salty ocean breeze and pure alpha maleness.

My knees nearly buckle. Fresh slick gushes between my thighs, and a wave of heat, so intense and painful I gasp, hits my core.

Two's head snaps toward me, his sensors immediately detecting the change. "Core temperature 41.7 degrees Celsius," he announces with clinical precision. "Beth, please return to the nest. Further knotting recommended."

Ace's nostrils flare, and for the first time, he reacts the way an alpha usually would to an omega in heat, spraying him with her horniness. He straightens slowly. His pupils fully dilate and go so white they completely overtake the beautiful blue irises. His muscles enlarge and his teeth bare.

But instead of jumping me, instead of advancing, he takes a deliberate step backward and says, "I should probably go," his voice lower, rougher.

I need to get away from this guy. I don't know how much longer I can stop myself from pouncing on him.

I realize in this moment that he, too, is fighting his urge to mate with me. Possibly has been this entire time.

Why? I don't know.

He turns, holding the surfboard against his erection and says, "But it was really nice meeting you, Styles. Your alphabots are amazing, but not as amazing as you."

The simple compliment, delivered with such guileless sincerity, hits me harder than any sophisticated flattery ever could.

Another wave of heat blasts through me, more intense than the last. A cramp with the fire of a thousand suns explodes in my uterus, sending intense heat through my limbs and down my legs...no, that's slick—more slick than I've ever produced in a single wave. The water bottle in my hand falls to the ground, emptying its contents into the sand.

I need to cool down.

"Water," I gasp, looking around for some.

There's some—a whole bunch.

My body moves on instinct, turning toward the ocean.

I need to cool down. Need to escape this confusing, overwhelming attraction.

"Beth?" Two asks, concern in his voice, as I stumble toward the waves.

Behind me, I hear Ace call out something, but the blood rushing in my ears and the crash of waves drown out his words.

All I know is that I need to get away.

I need to submerge myself in the cold ocean water.

I need to clear my head and make sense of why this simple-minded surfer has affected me so profoundly.

The water beckons, promising relief from the fire that consumes me from within.

5

ACE

The robot dudes' eyes are doing this weird zoomy, spinny thing as they watch Styles walk toward the water. They all follow her but don't close the distance. It's as if they're tethered to her by some invisible string. Maybe the same one that feels like it's pulling me toward her and killing me to keep taught.

That scent of hers wrapped around me like an invisible rope a mile out on the water and has been tugging at my heart and balls—but mostly my heart—ever since. I'm not known for my ability to focus, but it's made focusing damn near impossible.

I shake my head, forcing myself to concentrate, because something is wrong with her. She got all horny for me and then started walking toward the ocean.

The caring-looking robot, the one she called Two, said something about her temperature. What did he say?

"Hey, robot dude. What's her temperature again?" I ask, trying to keep my voice steady despite the rut burning through my veins.

He looks at me with those spinning mechanical eyes.

They're so cool and creepy. I want to poke them with a stick to see what happens.

Concentrate, Ace!

He says, "Beth's core temperature is 41.7 degrees Celsius."

Huh?

I ask, "Like, in normal numbers?"

Two's eyes stop whirling, and he responds, "Error. Normalization is undefined for a single scalar without context. The value provided is already an absolute physical measurement."

What the fuck does that mean?

"No! I mean, what is that in Fahrenheit? Um...approximately, don't give me a million decimal values."

"Approximately 107 degrees Fahrenheit."

Holy shit. That's way too high.

"That's like, brain-melting high," I say, my rut-fogged mind suddenly clearing with alarm. "Shouldn't you guys get her to her nest? Don't omegas need to, like, be in their nest to avoid injury during heat?"

They all reply in a creepy, synchronized way: "Now running: Nesting Sequence 23."

"So, um...take her to her nest then."

Two, who must be the brains of the operation, replies, "We cannot restrain Beth during heat cycles unless explicitly commanded. It violates Prime Directive Omega 1."

She's stumbling toward the ocean in nothing but a towel, her movements unsteady. I've wiped out enough times in cold water to know what happens when a body hits freezing waves, even without a fever—this is why you wear a wetsuit.

I don't wait to hear more. I drop my surfboard and sprint across the sand. "Hey, robot lady! Styles! Stop!" I shout. "That water is freezing. You'll go into shock!"

She doesn't turn. Maybe she can't hear me over the crashing waves. Maybe her fever's too high to process my words. Either way, she wobbles closer to the water.

I push harder. My muscles burn as my feet dig into the soft grains with each desperate stride. The rut gives me an extra surge of energy, fueling my body to fuck and fight, but right now, to protect.

This is my fault. I aroused her and fried that beautiful brain of hers.

So fucking stupid, Ace. You should have turned around the moment you smelled the fear wafting off her.

This wasn't the plan. The plan was to find the source of that perfect scent, drop myself a pin of her location, go home, masturbate furiously, and then come back in two weeks when she wasn't in heat anymore. Not stalkery...*well, not completely stalkery.*

I was going to come back and dangle my goods until she took the bait. Wait for her to come to me. You know, surf around all sexy-like, sit on the beach and flex as I wax my board, run my fingers through my hair, smile, and bend over in front of her. Basically, prance around like a gentleman peacock. *Hook, line, and sink into her.*

But the moment I realized the dudes she was fucking were robots, I had to talk to her. She was so fucking pretty, and the robots were so fucking cool. I just...couldn't help myself.

Goddamnit. Why do robots have to be so cool?!

I'm almost within reach of her. "Hey, Styles—"

A voice booms, "Potential threat detected. Protection Protocols activated," and something solid slams into my side, launching me a good ten feet in the opposite direction. I sprawl in the sand, dazed. *What the fuck was that?* It felt like I got hit with one of those giant metal balls on a rope that wreck things, that I can't remember the name of at the moment, because a swarm of bees is building a nest within my head, blacking my vision and ringing my ears.

My sight clears, and the robot that was locked in Styles's ass earlier, Alpha-3, is standing above me. His scowl has transformed into an even more fearsome sneer, accompanied by red glowing eyes. *He must be her guard dog.*

He booms, "Alpha, disengage your attempts to mate with the omega, Dr. Elizabeth Styles. Four non-lethal attacks remain before Deadly Force Protocols activate."

What the fuck? He's gonna kill me?

I try to scramble away from the menacing bot, but it's pointless;

my feet just dig into the sand, and I barely add any distance between us. "Isn't it like a robot law or something that you can't hurt people?"

He smirks. "My Primary Objectives are to fuck Elizabeth and fuck up any human alpha who tries to fuck her. And you appear to be trying to fuck my omega, alpha."

"What? No!" I shout and try to roll away, but I'm stopped by a grip so hard on my ankle that it feels like it might rip my flesh from my bones.

Alpha-1, the muscular one, whose expression until now always looked sweet and idiotic, has a firm grip on my ankle and is sneering at me with red eyes.

"I'm not trying to fuck her!" I yell to the brobots. "I'm trying to help her! She'll go into shock if she goes into that water with that fever!"

Elizabeth is a few steps away from the swash zone now.

Fuck, I'm going to have to fight these robots, aren't I? That's cool, but also...not cool!

I kick One's jealousy-inducing chest with my free foot, but it does nothing to break his grip. It may have broken my foot, though. These guys are strong—unnaturally strong. It's like trying to fight heavy machinery.

I desperately kick at his hand and arm, accidentally hitting my own leg in the process. He just tightens his grip. But I don't give up. I keep kicking, cutting my feet on his knuckles, and doing more damage to myself than him. Just as I think I might not have any kicks left in me, a blow connects at a spot on his wrist, loosening his grip just enough for me to wriggle free.

I spring to my feet, despite the throbbing in my newly freed leg and the sting of sand pressing into my foot's wounds. "Guys, seriously! She's going to hurt herself!"

Two's eyes also glow red, but his nice, caretaker expression remains. He takes a defensive stance between Elizabeth and me. "Your alpha rut pheromones paired with your insistent pursuit imply aggressive intent," he says calmly. "We cannot allow you to approach Dr. Elizabeth Styles. Please cease your attempts to harm our omega."

"No! I'm not trying to hurt her; I'm trying to help her!"

One launches at me. I twist away, ducking under his swinging arm and driving my elbow into his midsection. His synthetic skin feels almost human, but it crumples under the force. The hard metal of his internal workings connects at the exact point on my arm people call funny, but is anything but.

The sting radiates outward, shooting electrical pulses through my teeth and balls. I push through the pain and back away from him. I shout, "She needs help! Help her, idiots!"

One says, "We are helping. Rutting alpha in proximity of omega. Protection Protocols are in effect." It seems like maybe he's not just made to look dumb for aesthetics; this guy is an idiot.

While my eyes are locked on the beautiful dummy, a fist approaches my face in my periphery. I crouch just before it clocks me in the jaw. Thank God, because Three put so much force behind it, his body follows through with it. He falters slightly, but rights himself almost immediately.

Jesus Christ. Okay, she wasn't lying about their balance. These things could surf.

Two comes at me from the left. I drop low and sweep his legs, a move that would topple any human, but he barely stumbles. I, however, now have a second throbbing shin.

Elizabeth is at the water's edge now, and the towel slips from her shoulders. Her naked body gleams in the sunlight—beautiful and vulnerable in a way that makes my alpha instincts roar.

The distraction leaves me vulnerable, too.

Three grabs me from behind in a bear hug.

I try to launch my body forward and throw him off balance, but his grip is tight, and his stability was designed by a genius, so it doesn't work. I stomp hard on his foot. Nothing, not a peep—from him anyway—my foot screams in pain. I throw my head back, connecting with Three's face, but the only thing it accomplishes is an unnatural cracking sound that is more likely my skull splitting open than his face. My ears ring, and my vision blackens again.

Three's grip doesn't loosen; he's completely unaffected. Actually, that's not true. He squeezes me tighter.

He's not a human. I've gotta attack this thing like a machine, not a human with reflexes and stuff.

Alpha-3 exhales hot on my ear and growls, "Two non-lethal attacks remaining before activating deadly force. Disengage your attack sequence on Dr. Elizabeth Styles."

I'd be interested in knowing how this thing breathes if I weren't, you know, about to die. "What!? I thought I had four remaining!?"

He squeezes me tighter and says, all business, "I am required to attempt five non-lethal attacks before activating Deadly Force Protocols. I have implemented three total attacks. Body Slam Variation 2: Success. Right Hook Variation 1: Failure. Bear Hug Variation 4: Success."

"Look at her!" I shout at them, struggling in Three's grip. "She's about to pass out, and the water could kill her!"

Elizabeth's feet are in the surf now as she sways at the shoreline. A small wave splashes against her calves, and she jerks away, but doesn't retreat.

Fuck. Fuck. Fuck. Fuck.

I inspect Three's arms wrapped around my chest. *Is there an off switch for this guy or something? I have no idea how these fucking things work.*

I slam my uninjured elbow into the joints of his arm, hoping that's where the important bits are hidden within the creepily fake flesh.

After multiple painful—for me, not him—blows, his grip loosens enough for me to escape.

I must save my omega.

I feint left, then dive right, rolling past One as he charges at me.

I spring to my feet just a few yards from Elizabeth as she takes another unsteady step deeper into the water.

Two lunges for me, but I pivot.

Three and One lunge in a synchronized move, but I roll out of the way.

They're fast—but their movements are predictable, like bosses in a video game. Once I figure out their pattern, they're easy to avoid. I just gotta spam these rolls. While my maneuvers are excellently evasive, they aren't actually getting me any closer to Styles.

Suddenly, they shift, as if I've somehow triggered Phase 2 of this boss battle. Two moves between Elizabeth and me, and announces, "Rutting alpha within three meters of Dr. Elizabeth Styles."

The others circle me.

I'm surrounded.

Two says, "94% probability that you intend to mate with Dr. Elizabeth Styles against her will." He pauses, then tells the others, "Activate Deadly Force Protocol." A loud hissing noise emits from all of them, and they expand, as if their muscles are inflating with air. Two's pupils turn red, eyes now red on red, and his gaze burns into me, obviously locking onto his target. "Alpha, you have ten seconds to exit the perimeter before death." His expression is oddly serene despite the violence.

They raise their hands in a new fighting stance and count down in unison. "Ten. Nine..."

6

ACE

"I'm trying to save her life!" I roar, my patience snapping.

I drop my shoulder and barrel through Two with everything I have left in me. The impact jars every bone in my body. He shifts and stumbles back, but recovers quickly, his balance unbelievable.

He remains in the circle with the others. They're all looking at the spot I was a few seconds ago, and continue to count down. "Six. Five..." It's like they're stuck, unable to leave their position, until they finish the countdown.

I leap for Elizabeth, reaching her just as her knees buckle and the robots say, "Two. One."

I wrap my arms around her waist from behind, and pull her away from the water's edge.

She screams—a sound of pure terror that tears at my heart—and tries to wrench herself from my grip.

I let go immediately, stepping back with my hands raised.

"Please don't hurt me," she whimpers, falling to her knees in the wet sand. Her eyes are unfocused, glassy with fever. She curls in on herself, arms wrapped protectively around her body. The towel lies forgotten beside her.

The sight of her distress makes me want to punch myself in the face. Unfortunately, I'm not the only one who wants to hurt me right now.

"Rutting Alpha Extermination Sequence 13 activated," the three alphabots say in unison.

God, please don't tell me they can shoot lasers from their eyes or something.

"I'm not going to hurt you," I say, keeping my voice as gentle as I can despite the rut-rage still coursing through me and the murderous robots closing in on me.

I whisper, using the name that the robot—who looks sweet when he's not trying to kill me—calls her, "Beth, the water is freezing today. If you go in, you'll go into shock. Your temperature is way too high."

She blinks up at me, confusion clouding her beautiful, brilliant face. Her scent hits me again. But the coconut is accompanied not by freshly baked cookies, but cookies pulled from the oven, flaming and spoiled. She's terrified.

Even laced with fear, her scent is intoxicating, triggering thoughts like: *Mate. Mine. Protect. Claim. Mark.*

My mouth waters, and my teeth itch to claim her right here in the wet sand. I have to clench my fists to stay in control.

The alphabots are advancing, their synthetic bodies showing signs of damage. Three's face is partially caved in, revealing a complex metal skeleton beneath, making his menacing face even scarier. One's chest panel is dented, exposing wiring that sparks occasionally. Two looks like he might actually start shooting lasers at me—his eyes are red, his caring face grimaces murderously, and his leg is bent at a weird angle, dragging behind him.

"Please call off your alphabots before they kill me. I promise I'm just trying to help you," I say as calmly as I can.

Clarity hasn't fully returned to her emerald eyes yet, but they widen when she sees her broken bots. When her gaze comes back to me, I can't tell what scares her more: the damage to her robots or me.

"Your alphabots didn't try to stop you. I'm sorry. I had to stop you," I explain, taking another step back, fighting every instinct that screams at me to claim her, to cool her burning skin with my touch, to protect her from everything, including herself.

Alpha Two announces, "Step away from Dr. Eliz—"

"Alphabots, disengage all Deadly Force Sequences and Protection Protocols," Elizabeth shouts just before they reach me, likely about to snap my neck.

They stop instantly, and the red hue of their eyes go back to a more natural-looking color.

Her gaze returns to them, likely assessing the damage, but she doesn't say anything.

"I'm sorry I damaged your bots," I tell her, backing up even further until there's at least ten feet between us. "And I'm really sorry I scared you. I just couldn't let you go into that water. You could have died."

She still doesn't say anything. She just looks down at her hand, squeezing her fingers in the sand.

The rut screams within me: *Care. Love. Comfort.*

"I'll pay for repairs," I promise quickly. "Whatever they cost. I'm so sorry."

Elizabeth makes a slight, broken sound as tears stream down her face.

My heart twists painfully in my chest; each tear feels like a pair of hands wringing it.

These fucking machines! This is their fault!

"What kind of alpha wouldn't protect their omega?!" I demand, unable to keep the growl from my voice. "You were just going to let her walk into freezing water with a raging fever! You assholes don't deserve to call yourselves alphabots!"

Alpha-2 steps forward, his movements slightly jerky from the damage to his leg. "Our programming does not allow us to restrain Beth during her heat cycles unless explicitly commanded. This is Prime Directive Omega 1. It overrides all other Protocols except those pertaining to immediate life-threatening situations."

"Walking into freezing water with a 107-degree fever is life-threatening!" I argue.

One moves beside Two, adding, "We are not to restrain," he pauses, then smiles, saying, "Sunshine, when Heat Protocols are activated."

He is the dumb one.

A small voice says, "It's not their fault."

My attention turns to Elizabeth. Her voice cracks, and she adds, "It's mine. It's my fault. It's my shitty code." Her shoulders shake with sobs, and she looks so small, so vulnerable.

I want to go to her, wrap her in my arms, and tell her everything will be okay, but the fear still wafts off her in waves, mingling with her heat scent in a combination that makes my stomach churn.

Whatever drove this beautiful genius to build these bots to avoid interacting with alphas during heat—whatever drove her to write code that wouldn't let them restrain her no matter what—is also driving her to recoil whenever I move.

So instead of going to her, I sit down heavily in the sand, making myself smaller, less threatening. "Hey," I say softly. "Your code isn't shitty."

"Yes, it is. It was stupid of me to think I could account for every scenario."

"Stupid? Elizabeth, you are far from stupid. Your code isn't shitty. Look at those things. I don't know shit about robots, but I know that's amazing! I bet no one else has made bots that cool."

She looks at them and grimaces. They flinch, as if the disgust on her face affects them the same way it affects me.

"Code can be fixed, right? Nobody gets it perfect the first time. Isn't that why you were doing a test run?" I ask, knowing full well that wasn't a test run. "So you can find the things to fix? So you can collect data and then, like, make changes?"

She looks up, surprise flickering across her tear-streaked face. Her lips twitch slightly, not quite a smile but close.

I'm not sure why what I'm saying is reaching through her fear and heat delirium, but it is, so I'm gonna keep at it until she feels better. I want to see her smile.

"Didn't you say they learned stuff?" I continue. "Now they learned they can't let you run into water."

She chuckles, just a little, but a smile doesn't crack her face.

I add with my own chuckle, "And they learned that their fighting skills need some work."

She laughs again, harder this time, so I keep at it. "I know a genius like you probably doesn't fail often, but take it from me, I fail a lot. Learning through failure is one of the best ways to learn. I bet these amazing bots with your genius code learn even better than knotheads like me."

She turns to me, and a genuine smile pulls at her face.

Then, suddenly, her eyes roll back, and she slumps forward.

I move reflexively, lifting to my feet and crossing the distance between us in two strides. I catch her before she hits the sand.

As my arms wrap around her, her scent envelops me completely: coconut with a hint of vanilla and something uniquely her—like the best cookies you've ever smelled baking in the oven, no longer tainted with fear.

My rut responds: a tsunami of oceanic lust and protective possessiveness rushes out of me. My scent reaches out to hers. They ebb and flow together as if they were made for this dance.

Scent-matched...

This is my omega. Mine. My fate.

I must help her.

Her flesh against mine burns hot, like sand at noon on a beach.

I've never been with an omega in heat before, but I know the basics. They get super hot and super horny. You gotta fuck 'em, keep 'em cool and hydrated, and cuddle 'em in their nests. Every alpha I know has had this information drilled into their head since they were old enough to know they were an alpha. That way, even the dumbest of us will know what to do, no matter how rutting dumb we are.

I want to take her to her nest and rut into her so good I scramble those brilliant, beautiful brains as if my dick were a spatula. I'm not as smart as she is, but I'm not dumb enough to do that. She doesn't want me; she wants them...

The alphabots creep toward us, their damage more significant than I realized.

Can they do all of that for her? Can they really take care of her now that I've broken them?

I growl at these fucking bots.

How dare they let me damage them?!

These fuckers should have saved her. They should have killed me. They should have done a million things other than what they did.

Their eyes aren't red, but they do look like they are going to attack me again—probably still calculating how to rip her from my arms so they can pummel me properly.

They're not alphas. They're alphabots. They follow rules. Rules that she laid out for them.

Maybe if I speak their language, I can get through to them.

What was it they said earlier?

I say, stilting my voice in a calm robo-y way, "Omega cannot walk without assistance. Ummm...my Nesting Sequence 1 is activated. Um...my Primary Direction is to save Dr. Elizabeth Style's life through temperature management, by getting her to her nest and not —repeat, not—rutting into her."

I grimace. *That was fucking stupid. They're gonna kill me now.*

Two's eyes whirl, and he says, "61% probability that alpha will take Beth to her nest without incident."

Wow, I'm happy to inspire such confidence.

Two commands, "Activate Nesting Sequence 30," then he and Three walk away.

One approaches, grabs the discarded towel, says, "Follow us, Alpha-Ace," then follows the others toward her house.

Okay, so I guess my plan worked.

I cradle Elizabeth carefully against my chest and follow them.

I look down at her face, peaceful now in unconsciousness. Her blonde hair falls across her forehead in damp tendrils, and her lips are slightly parted. She's the most beautiful thing I've ever seen.

Mine.

The word echoes through me with absolute certainty. This brilliant, vulnerable woman is my mate. I've never been more sure of anything in my life.

As I follow the alphabots with now jerky movements but still impeccable balance toward her home, I make a silent promise to the woman in my arms and myself:

I'll take care of her.

I'll do for her what these bots can't—what that is, I don't know yet.

I'll protect her better than any robot ever could.

I'll earn her trust.

I'll help her heal whatever wounds made her build these things in the first place.

7
ACE

A disembodied voice says, "Welcome home, Dr. Styles," as the doors automatically slide open.

Whoa, that's cool.

"How does it do that? How did it know to open?" I ask the bot nearest me.

"The house is programmed to recognize Beth's biometrics and react accordingly," Two answers.

I step inside the darkened home, and dim lights illuminate the space. The interior steals my breath. The ceiling soars two stories high, and everything is sleek, minimalist, and super high-tech.

"Whoa," I breathe, shifting Elizabeth's weight carefully and walking forward. Lights turn on with each step I take as I follow the bots, revealing more of the house to me. "She actually lives here?"

Across the ample living space, a stairwell curves as if suspended by magic. Behind it, a waterfall cascades down glass to a pond below —golden koi shimmer and move within it.

"Holy shit," I whisper.

The open floor plan reveals a kitchen with so much machinery it looks like an assembly line on a fancy factory floor. Multiple pairs of robotic arms, mounted along a rail system, sit folded—awaiting their instructions, I suppose. The rails weave through the ceiling, handleless cabinets, and light stone counters—counters that are so sleek and precise I suspect any germ attempting to adhere to their surfaces would just slide right off.

I note other signs of robotics throughout the living space: rails tucked neatly against the floorboards, small machines whose functions I couldn't begin to fathom, and dimmed-screen panels built within surfaces.

I follow the bots up the stairs and adjust my grip on Elizabeth as we ascend, hyper-aware of her vulnerable form in my arms.

I love fish, so I sneak a glance over the stair rails into the pond. Their colors all shift from gold to orange and white, stopping me in my tracks, and I blink to make sure my eyes aren't playing tricks on me.

Holy shit. They're robots, too! Fucking amazing.

The moment I reach the top of the stairs, a hallway illuminates, stretching before us.

The bots, thoroughly unimpressed by their environment, walk to the end of the hall at a perfectly steady pace. They stop at the last door on the right, and all turn to me with creepy synchronicity.

"This is Beth's nest chamber," Two reports.

I nod, and he opens the door, standing back with the others to let me enter first.

I step through, then freeze, certain we've entered some portal to another home.

This isn't the sterile, high-tech space I expected. This is...pink. So pink. And fluffy. I wriggle my toes in the plush carpeting as I take the place in with all my senses.

Every shade of pink, all of which I don't know the name for, fills the large circular room. A pale fabric cascades down the walls in gentle waves, and tiny lights twinkle on the ceiling.

The nest is an enormous, round bed in the center of the room. It's a mountain of pillows, blankets, and stuffed animals—all appear impossibly soft and impossibly pink. The only hard surfaces in the space are the wall panels that light up as I approach, displaying charts and data I don't understand.

I look down at Elizabeth, then back at the room, trying to reconcile the woman I met on the beach, the woman who lives in the sleek, high-tech house, with the omega who rides out her heat in a cotton-candy dreamland.

"This is her nest?" I manage, finally.

"Yes," Alpha-2 replies.

I imagine her here alone, nestled in this pink nest, purring herself to sleep surrounded by robots she built to avoid human contact. Something soft and protective expands in my chest. I step carefully toward the nest, overwhelmed by tenderness. "She's like two different people," I murmur.

"Error. Styles is one person," One says, looking at me with a face that reads as confusion but probably means, "collecting data," which I suppose is probably the same thing with these guys.

"No, I mean, this nest seems like it belongs to another person."

One looks to the room, and the mechanics in his chest make a slight grinding noise. He tilts his head, simulating dumbness. "But only one person lives in this establishment." His damaged chest panel tightens up as if his thinking happens there. *Maybe it does. I dunno how these fuckers work.*

"Never mind, dude," I say as I gently lay Elizabeth in her nest. I arrange her limbs in a way that I hope is comfortable and then cover her nudity with a nearby blanket, careful not to touch anything unnecessarily.

I brush back the hair that has fallen across her eyes. Her fever is raging, hot against my fingers, and her cheeks are flushed.

Her blonde hair fans out over a bright pink pillow, contrasting in a way that makes her look like a princess awaiting her true love's kiss. I do my best to repress the scent that wants to explode out of me at the sight. I can't leave any unwelcome traces of myself—intruding on an omega's nest and leaving your scent in it may as well be the eighth deadly sin.

She doesn't look comfortable enough...

Something inside me says, *'Wrap your omega in their nest as if they're a fragile gift in a world that aggressively shakes its presents.'* I don't know if I just came up with that or if some instructor drilled it into my head years ago, but I follow its instructions.

I scan the mountain of blankets and pillows. "Which does she like best?" I ask the bots as my hands hover uncertainly over the various textures. "How does she like to be nestled?"

"The blue weighted blanket provides optimal pressure," Two answers from the doorway. "The faux fur pillows should be positioned around her head. The microfleece blanket with a cloud pattern goes over her lower body."

I follow the directions, carefully tucking the weighted blanket around her shoulders, arranging the impossibly soft faux fur pillows, and draping the cloud blanket over her legs.

She sighs in her sleep, turning to press her face into one of the furry pillows. Her coconut scent intensifies, shifting to contented pleasure.

Heat floods my system in response.

Mine. Mate. Breed. Bond.

I force myself to step back, putting distance between us before I do something stupid like climb into the nest with her and hug her face to my chest.

I turn to the alphabots, still hovering near the doorway, making no move to join her.

"What are you guys waiting for?" I ask, gesturing toward Elizabeth. "Don't tell me she hasn't programmed you to cuddle."

Alpha-2 announces to no one in particular, "Omega in nest. Activate Repair Prioritization Protocols."

They turn and limp through the doorway.

"Where are you going?" I ask them in disbelief.

They stop and turn in another synchronized move that creeps me out, but only Two responds. "We are retiring to the laboratory to receive repairs. Alpha, please follow us out of the nest."

I stare at them. "Are you joking? She needs you right now."

They all look at me as if registering my words, then toward Elizabeth in her nest. Their eyes whirl, reminding me once again that they are not human.

Alpha-2 speaks for them. He says simply, "No. Only Alpha-1 has Joking Modules installed."

Elizabeth whimpers, hugging her knees to her chest.

Oh, sweetheart, I'll fix it...I'm here.

My body lurches toward her, arms outstretched to hug her.

No! I can't.

I am not her pack. These mecha meatheads are.

"So you're just going to leave her like this?" I ask in disbelief. "Don't you have, like, an Aftercare Module or something?"

Alpha-2's eyes whirl again, and he responds. "If our bodies receive structural damage, our instructions require we await repairs."

Fuck, these guys are really getting on my nerves.

"What kind of alphas are you?" The words come out as a growl, my rut-enhanced protectiveness flaring hot and bright.

"Alphabots," One adds unhelpfully.

Two adds, "Repair Prioritization Protocol is activated—"

"Yeah, yeah, your protocols," I cut him off, pacing the soft carpet. "You know what? Your protocols suck. No real alpha would abandon their omega during heat just because they got a little banged up."

"We are alphabots," One adds again, and I want to punch him in his beautiful dumb face just to shut him up, but I know it will just break my hand, so I don't.

Three crosses his arms, appearing intimidating and aloof at the same time, as he leans in the doorway. "Are you questioning our omega's programming ability, alpha?" He smirks, and his mangled face somehow adds to the schoolyard bully aesthetic.

"No...I just..." I trail off and turn back to Elizabeth, who shifts and whimpers again. I run a hand through my hair, as guilt and frustration wage war inside me. "Fuck. You can't just leave her like this."

"Core Directive Sigma 2 dictates we must ensure our bodies are not damaged when entering the nest," Two states flatly. "It is a core directive. So I have activated the Repair Prioritization Protocols."

A soft, angelic purr comes from the nest, and my head whips toward Elizabeth. Omegas only purr in the most distressing, desperate times. She's shivering, trying to comfort herself.

I'm coming! Let me make it better, babygirl!

My purr responds, a mind of its own, ceasing her purr, but I have to stop my body from following suit. I can't go to her.

But these fuckers can!

I turn back to the alphabots, unable to stop the anger escaping me in a bark. "SHE NEEDS HER PACK! HELP HER!"

The bark does nothing, which makes sense, they're glorified dildos.

Two tilts his head at me, as if he's about to explain something to a child, and sighs. He softens his voice and says, "Core Direct—"

"I get it!" I whisper-shout, cutting him off, barely repressing the rage in my voice. I'm so fucking angry at these droid dorks, I might actually fight them again.

We're just talking in circles.

This is ridiculous. An omega with a whole pack of alphas should never have to purr for themselves—

But wait...

She doesn't have a pack. She's got sex toys with faces. They don't think—not really. They follow directions. They follow rules.

Rules she wrote.

Think. Think, Ace.

Fuck. Of all the alphas in the world, I'm probably the last you'd choose to outthink a robot, but I have no choice right now...

They said something about prime directives earlier. I have no idea what a prime directive is or if it's different from a core directive. I also have no idea what the difference is between a directive and a protocol, or how these bots make decisions...

But prime sounds important. And if a prime directive is like a Prime Alpha, it should have authority over a core directive, right?

"Isn't taking care of your omega during heat a Prime Directive? Wouldn't that outrank a core directive or protocol or whatever?" I ask, having no idea what the fuck I'm talking about.

They all look at me with blank, whirling eyes, like they're looping through some decision process.

Shit, am I getting through to them?

I wait for them to respond.

And wait...

And wait...

My relief transforms to impatience, then panic, because they're still doing it—too long. It's like they'll be looking for the answer to my question forever.

Are their brains going to explode?

Did I accidentally ask them to divide by zero like one of those robots in that movie I saw?

Fuck! Did I break them? AGAIN?

"Never mind," I say, waving my hand in front of their faces, breaking them out of the brain-melting sequence I suspect I triggered with my question.

Two states, "Alpha, please leave the nest—"

"You guys are really starting to piss me off," I mutter, pacing again. "What would happen if I just ordered you to stay here and help her?"

Their posture changes, and they look like they might start fighting me again.

Or pull out those lasers that I suspect they have hidden within their heads.

"You do not have authorization to override our Protocols," Two explains in an inflexible tone. "Only Dr. Elizabeth Styles can modify our Core Directives."

Three smirks, crosses his arms again, then says, "Sorry, alpha, but you can't make us do shit." The damage to his jaw exposes the tongue in his mouth just enough for me to notice that it doesn't move when he talks. *It must just be used for sexy stuff.*

I stare at them, out of ideas, and size up their damage. *They have to be repaired. I guess there's no getting around it.* Their logic is as inflexible as the hard metal within their bodies.

Oh, hold on. I get it.

Their damage gave them all weird, sharp edges in different places. If they got in the nest with her, they'd probably hurt her. So, I guess this protocol or directive or whatever makes sense.

I tug my hair in frustration. The alphabots stand motionless, waiting, probably only programmed to tell me to leave a certain number of times to save battery or something.

"Fine," I say with a defeated sigh. "Go get your repairs. But hurry the hell up. I'll stay here and keep an eye on her."

Alpha-2 sizes me up with those whirling eyes. "We cannot permit that. Your rut pheromones are at critical levels. Proximity to Dr. Elizabeth Styles in her current state presents a high risk of—"

"I'm not going to touch her," I interrupt, my voice hard with certainty. "I'll sit right here by the door. But someone needs to monitor her fever, and since you three are abandoning her for the robot hospital, that someone is me."

"Protection Proto—" Three begins.

"FINE!" I snap. "I will wait in the living room. Go repair yourselves. The sooner you get fixed, the sooner you can actually help her."

The alphabots exchange glances—an oddly human gesture—before nodding in unison.

Two says, his voice almost conveying shame, which seems weird, "We do not have the programming to repair ourselves."

"Oh, my fucking God. You've got to be joking."

One smiles and spreads his arms, saying, "An alpha walked into a bar—"

I cut him off. "No jokes!"

One looks sad for a moment, like he was excited to tell me a joke, and I feel a little bad about it. Luckily, he returns to his normal, sexy, and dumb expression pretty quickly.

Two adds, "We must await repairs."

Well, fuck. There's only one person who can repair them, and she can't right now. She must have some failsafes or whatever for this, right? I wish I could ask her. I wish I were smart enough to help her... but I'm not. I'm a beautiful idiot, just like One. *Well, maybe not as dumb as One...*

I watch the gorgeous genius reach for her stuffed animals in her nest, pulling them toward her to hug.

Mine.

It would be so easy to climb into that nest with her. To fix what ails her with my knot...

Even if she could consent to my help right now, I'm pretty sure she wouldn't. She built robots specifically to avoid having a real alpha touch her during heat. She didn't say it, but it's pretty obvious.

I'm no one to her. I'm just a stranger who crashed her automated orgy on the beach and broke her expensive sex robots.

All of this is my fault.

I have to fix this. I have to fix them.

I ask Two, "Okay, what needs to happen for you to get in that nest and take care of her? What kind of repairs are we talking about?"

"Structural damage must be mended," Alpha-2 explains.

"Does she have, like, tools to fix you somewhere?"

Two nods. "Beth has a repair station in her laboratory."

I take a deep breath, fighting the urge to punch something—preferably not a robot. "Where's the laboratory?"

"The laboratory is on the lowest level."

"Show me where this repair station is."

8
STYLES

I wake to the gentle vibrations of my alphabots purring in perfect harmony. All three of my alphabots are holding me—something they haven't done since early testing phases.

I pull a fluffy pillow to my face and nuzzle into it, only to notice there's a leg attached to it. Well, a synthetic leg.

What the fuck?

I pull back, blinking as my eyes adjust to the soft lighting of my nest.

Two, whose leg I'm currently gripping, leans down to brush hair from my face, saying, "You're awake."

How did I get in my nest?

One and Three are still in Standby Mode, but their purrs have remained on—something else they haven't done since early testing.

I shift, lifting onto my elbows to look at the bots. Silver, blue, and neon pink strips of duct tape intricately crisscross their bodies, securing stuffed animals and pillows in place, effectively mummifying their limbs.

They've been vandalized!

I gasp, and Three flies upward, duct tape haphazardly covering his face, holding a pink unicorn to his jaw. "Who hurt you? I will kill them!" he says, his eyes turning red as he boots directly into Guard Mode from Standby Mode. "Deadly Force Protocols are activated."

One blinks, his older, slower processors booting up less quickly, and says, "Confused. Does Sunshine require oral stimulation, protection, or continued purring?"

Two's eyes whirl, scanning me for signs of distress. "No threat detected. Beth was simply startled by our appearance."

What...what is happening? They never immediately boot into specific modes after being on Standby.

"Understood," Three says, as his eyes return to their normal hue and his posture shifts to that devil-may-care, arm-on-knee lean that makes him look like he's modeling designer underwear—which he kind of is. But his current condition downgrades the pose in an almost comedic way. The arm draped over his knee is splinted with a pillow. His expression, which should be sultry and rebellious, is transformed into something more like what you'd see on a rodeo clown by the duct tape and unicorn locking his jaw in place.

One is in a similar condition. His chest panel is sealed shut with what looks like an entire roll of industrial-strength silver tape and a giant teddy bear. His arm is also splinted with a pillow.

Two got the least of it, and it appears his only major alteration is the pillow attached to his leg with a massive amount of tape.

"What happened to you?" I whisper, as a strange, inappropriate urge to laugh bubbles up inside me as I take in more of this bizarre art project inflicted upon my bots.

They look ridiculous—my perfect, precision-engineered alphabots reduced to duct-taped disasters.

Two answers: "Alpha-Ace administered emergency repairs to our bodies."

Alpha-Ace?

I lie back down. My head is still a little heat-fuzzy, but fragments of memory cascade through my mind.

The beach.
The surfer.
Golden skin and salty ocean scent.
So fucking sexy.
Heat rising.
Stumbling toward water.

"The surfer did this to you?" I ask One as I trace the tape crossing his chest.

"Yes, Sunshine. Alpha-Ace broke me, then fixed me," One replies with a smile. "I like him. Can I keep the teddy bear? I like him, too. You hug me tighter with it."

"He broke you," I murmur to myself as another memory surfaces:

Cold shock against my calves.
Dizziness.
The world tilts.
'Please call off your alphabots...'
Brilliant smile.
'Your code isn't shitty.'

I turn to Two, because One is definitely not the one to ask questions about the chain of events that led up to this moment. "This was him...fixing you?" I can't keep the incredulity out of my voice.

Two shifts beside me, his tone maintaining its soothing Aftercare Profile. "Affirmative. He implemented temporary solutions to repair our damage until our status was sufficient to deactivate our Repair Prioritization Protocols. We were then able to implement Nesting Sequence 31 at 93% satisfaction despite the damage to our bodies."

I blink, unsure I heard him correctly. We haven't gotten numbers like that since the first heat Alpha-3 participated in. "Two, status report on most recent Nesting Sequence."

Two replies, "Nesting Sequence 31 lasted 5.34 hours. Historical satisfaction levels for Nesting Sequence 31 have resulted in 76%

satisfaction. However, once we implemented the adjustments recommended by Alpha-Ace to Aftercare Procedures satisfaction rose to 93%. I have updated Nesting Sequence 31 and Aftercare Procedures to include these adjustments for future implementations."

Adjustments?

I look around my nest, noticing more details now. My unicorn plushie—the one not taped to Three's face—is nestled perfectly against my side along with my pillows. My cloud-patterned throw is draped over my legs rather than tucked around them. But, most interestingly, my weighted blanket is against my shoulders and pelvis, but not my arms. I'm cradled and comforted, but not restrained. I can move easily and comfortably—something I didn't realize I wanted until this moment. Everything is situated in a way I've never tried but somehow feels strangely perfect.

"My nest items," I say slowly. "They're arranged differently."

"Yes," One confirms. "Alpha-Ace implemented his Nesting Sequence 1."

A spike of anxiety shoots through me at the thought of a stranger in my nest with me. "He was in my nest?"

"Negative," Two answers. "He entered the nesting chamber, but not the nest. He informed us of our improper nest material arrangements and suggested changes. We tested his suggestions and found your response optimal."

I blink, surprised. "It's nice. I would not have considered this."

Two nods. "The alpha demonstrated significant knowledge of omega comfort techniques. He identified optimal nest arrangements that resulted in an immediate 57% increase in satisfactory vitals. I predict the changes have decreased the total length of your heat cycle by at least eight hours. You are now in the final stages of this cycle."

A strange feeling unfurls in my chest—something warm and unfamiliar. My mouth quirks into a half-smile that could probably rival Three's when he doesn't have a unicorn strapped to his face.

This stranger, this surfer named Ace, saved me from potential shock and hypothermia, made sure my bots could help me through my heat flare, and also arranged my nest materials in a configuration I never would have tried but somehow feels perfect against my recovering body.

This is most perplexing.

"Where is he now?" I ask, surprised by my own curiosity.

"Pacing in the main living area," Two answers. "He's been waiting for you to wake."

He's been waiting over five hours for me?

There's that strange feeling unfurling in my chest again. I press my palm to my breast, noting the pounding of my heart and the smile I can't seem to repress.

"Would you like me to expel him from the residence?" Three asks, his damaged face trying to smirk.

"No," I giggle at the sight of the unicorn bouncing off his jaw as he tries to appear menacing.

Three says, attempting an uncharacteristic and unsuccessful pout, "But killing rutting alphas is my job."

Two adds, "His rut pheromones have increased by approximately 247% during his stay, but he has maintained a safe distance as requested. He does not appear to be a threat to Beth's safety. You cannot kill him."

One adds, "Alpha-Ace is no threat to Sunshine. He thinks she is his mate. He will not harm her. I like Alpha-Ace."

"What?"

Two answers: "His hormone levels indicate an emotional attachment to you."

One adds, "He also called Sunshine his omega." His eyes whirl, and then he reaches into his chest cavity under the teddy bear attached to it. In Ace's recorded voice, One says, "You guys have a lot to learn about being alphas. I will wait for her to wake up because I don't trust you robo-fuckers with my omega."

His omega?

A warm and gooey feeling floods me.

Two's eyes whirl as he assesses me. "What would you like us to do with Alpha-Ace?"

What would I like them to do, indeed?

An alpha who fights robots to save an omega, then fixes those same robots so they can care for her. An alpha who arranges a nest without entering it, who waits patiently while in rut for hours, only to pace with concern.

I've never encountered anything like this in any of my research.

The warm feeling in my chest expands, competing with the analytical part of my brain that insists this alpha is an unknown variable, potentially dangerous.

"I think," I say slowly, "I should probably thank him."

9
STYLES

My knees weaken, and I brace myself against the wall to stop myself from falling.

His scent. Oh, God, his scent. It's like a rogue wave of sexiness: powerful, overwhelming, and fuckable. It's as if an ocean storm—salt and ozone, raw energy, and untamed power—has been contained within the walls, and I just walked into it.

I take a deep breath, because it's all I can really do, and steady myself.

Three loops his arm under mine, providing support so I can walk down the remainder of the hallway.

At the top of the stairs, I break away from Three's embrace and peer down at Ace. He's pacing back and forth in the living room, visibly churning the air with his anxious movements. His rut pheromones circle him as if he's the eye of his own personal typhoon. They combine with the olfactory representation of his anxiety, but it too is visible: sloshing waves at his feet and an electrical storm at his head.

Fascinating, beautiful, and weirdly...not terrifying.

I've never been able to see someone's scent before—not even my own. *This is most peculiar. Why can I see it?*

He hasn't noticed me yet, too caught up in his restless movement, so I take this moment to leer at him. He's wearing what appears to be a pair of One's grey sweatpants. They're rolled up to his knees and hide nothing. His chest is bare, tanned, stretched over clearly defined muscles. His hair has dried in messy waves, and he's running his hands through it repeatedly, mussing it further.

Holy shit. He's striking.

He's so fucking beautiful, electricity jolts through my body at the sight of him, as if struck by the squall above his head.

I should be terrified—an unknown alpha in rut, in my home, while I'm still technically in heat. He's the personification of everything I try to avoid, but...even with the tempestuous storm raging around him, I'm not afraid. Not even a little. I'm drawn to him as if I were a storm chaser.

Why? What is happening to me?

I descend the stairs, gripping the rail, afraid I'll tumble down them otherwise. I can't break my eyes from him, even as the stairwell curves me away from him. I'm at the bottom of the steps before he even notices me.

He sniffs the air, turns, and his eyes meet mine.

The change is immediate and overwhelming. His nervous movements stop. His pupils dilate and cloud white. The scent storm around him drops—as if the air tilts and empties a sudden cascade of water—transforming the raging ocean into gentle waves on a warm summer day. The electricity remains, but softens to a pleasant buzz rather than threatening thunder.

"You're awake," Ace breathes, his voice deep and rich. "Are you okay?"

Heat floods through me—not the painful burn that usually accompanies my heat, but something warm and liquid, pooling low in my abdomen. My mind struggles to categorize the feeling washing over me—it's not just arousal, though that's certainly present. The intensity makes me stumble, my foot missing the last step.

He moves with surprising speed, crossing the room to catch me before I can fall, before my bots above me have even registered that I am falling. His arms wrap around my waist, strong and secure, and a rumbling purr starts in his chest.

I don't think I've ever felt a real alpha purr before—though, this feels familiar, as if it came to me in a dream. *Did he purr for me while I was asleep?* It's a sound so natural and perfect that it makes the alphabots' mechanical version seem hollow in comparison.

"I've got you, Cookie," he murmurs against my hair, breathing me in.

Cookie?

The purr vibrates through me, and I should pull away.

Internally, I'm screaming: *Back up. Establish distance. Don't touch him.*

But my body refuses to listen.

Instead, I lean into him, my face turning instinctively toward his neck, where his scent is most potent.

And when I inhale him from the source, I go boneless, weightless—floating in warm ocean waters.

Safe. Secure. Lucky he's holding on to me, or I'd drift away in the pleasure of his scent.

I feel safe in a way I've never experienced before. It makes absolutely no sense.

Three states, "Alpha touching omega without consent. Deadly Force Proto—"

Ace's purr deepens, and his arms tighten around me. "Oh, Cookie. You smell so good," he says, his voice strained. "Can you call off your boybots, though? They're about to murder me."

With my nose still pressed against Ace's skin, I command, "Alphabots, disengage Deadly Force Protocols until further notice. Alpha Ace is no threat."

"I dunno, Cookie. It's taking everything in me not to pick you up and carry you back to that pink fluffy room and eat you up," Ace sighs dreamily.

His honesty leaves me like my bots: disarmed. My lips part

slightly, and before I can process what I'm doing, my cheek is rubbing against his neck, marking him with my scent.

Ace moans. His hands are still gripped tight around me, but they remain respectfully at my waist, not wandering.

I want them to roam across the entire terrain of my body—like waves washing over the landscape during a flash flood.

But he doesn't ravish me as if he were a natural disaster; instead, he says, "I'm pretty sure you don't normally scent-mark random surfer dudes you just met. So maybe we should, like, take a step back? Before I do something stupid like try to knot you against that super cool waterfall wall thing?"

I want to be offended by his bluntness. But I'm not.

I want to recoil, then slap him for his explicit reference to knotting me. But I can't.

I'm charmed. Besotted. Fucking twitterpated. Enchanted by his transparency and complete lack of pretense or manipulation. And, if I'm being honest, I really want him to knot me against that waterfall.

I finally make myself pull back, breaking from his arms, but my fingers linger against his skin for a fraction of a second too long. The loss of contact sends a ripple of displeasure through me.

It's nothing. Just a standard biological response of an omega's heat calling to compatible alpha pheromones.

I clear my throat and say in an overly formal way, "Thank you for your assistance."

Should I shake his hand? No, that would be weird.

I add, righting myself and clearing my throat again. "For saving me from hypothermia and helping repair the alphabots."

Ace runs a hand through his hair, the movement causing another wave of his calming ocean scent to wash over me. "No problem, Cookie. I'm just glad you're okay." He backs away toward the couch, allowing me and my alphabots to finish our descent down the stairs unblocked.

"Why do you keep calling me Cookie?" I ask, tasting the nickname.

He grins, and the simple expression transforms his entire face. "Coconut cookies. The best kind."

I grin in response, unable to stop myself, as I settle into the space next to my robo-koi pond. The ridiculous nickname would annoy me under usual circumstances, but it appears I am in the most unusual circumstances.

"Your core temperature has increased by 0.4 degrees," Two observes from behind me. "Recommend maintaining distance from alpha pheromone source."

I nod, taking another deliberate step back even as my body protests.

Ace nods as well and glances toward the door, his expression conflicted. "I should probably get going. I didn't want to leave until you were lucid again. But...this rut isn't going to get any easier to control. Especially when...you smell like the most delicious..." He trails off, swallowing hard.

Like coconut cookies.

I'm surprised by how much I like his ridiculous food-based description of my scent. And I'm even more surprised that I haven't asked him to stop calling me Cookie yet.

He backs away further, thumbing at my kitchen. "Um, I ate some of your food. Sorry, rut makes alphas super hungry. You can, um...add the food to my probably already huge tab. Your kitchen is awesome, by the way. God, you're so fucking smart."

I blush. I know I'm smart—it's, like, my whole thing—but something about him appreciating it makes me feel all gooey inside. "You don't have to pay me back for the food. Or the bot damage. I'm grateful for your help."

He rubs his neck and nods. "Anyway," he continues, not meeting my eyes. "I should definitely leave before I do something stupid."

...like rut me against my waterfall...

His scent shifts again, the calm sea developing undercurrents of reluctance—which doesn't make any sense. *How can a scent convey reluctance?* I've always been terrible at reading people, but something about his scent just makes sense to me.

I'm probably misreading him just like I misread everyone. I'm lured into a false sense of understanding due to the familiarity of the scent—that's it.

But...his body language seems to mirror that interpretation.

He's shifting from foot to foot. His eyes are darting between me and the door. He's flexing his hands at his side.

He doesn't want to go.

The realization hits me with unexpected force, followed immediately by an even more surprising thought: *I don't want him to go either.*

This makes no sense. I designed my entire life—this house, my alphabots, my work schedule—around avoiding exactly this type of biological complication. Avoiding people. Avoiding alphas. *Especially alphas.*

Real alphas are unpredictable, demanding, and intrusive.

Violent.

Yet here I am, searching for reasons to keep this particular alpha in my space.

"So," Ace says, now at the door and breaking my train of thought. He gestures toward my alphabots, with their ridiculous duct-tape patches. "Are these guys going to be able to take care of you? For the rest of your, um, heat cycle? Because, no offense to your amazing robots, but they kinda look like they're held together with tape and hope right now."

I turn to assess my alphabots. Other than looking absurd, I do think they have some internal damage. They should have caught me as I fell down those stairs, and their purrs earlier seemed to function at reduced capacity.

Two steps forward, his movements slightly jerky. "Beth's heat has less than forty-eight hours remaining. Our current operational capacity is at 64.7%, which is sub-optimal for Complete Heat

Management but sufficient for implementing 72.3% of relevant sequences and routines."

Ace asks, "Is that a yes?"

Yes, it is. But I don't want it to be.

"No—" I begin to say, but Two speaks over me, saying, "Yes. Alpha-Ace can leave with confidence that Beth will be taken care of for the remainder of her heat."

"Two, I will handle further communication with Alpha-Ace," I nearly hiss at him.

I want Ace to stay.

What logical reason could I have to ask him to stay?

Ace's ocean scent shifts, and I swear it smells like tears—as if the ocean isn't composed of salt water, but the tears of countless souls wailing from the pain of limerence.

He smiles, but it's tight, and even I can tell it's fake when he says, "Well, great. I suppose I'll be going then. See you around, robot lady—Cookie—Styles."

But before he can dip out the door and out of my life forever, I shout, "Ace, wait!"

Fuck. What do I say now?

I stopped him without thinking it through. But I can't let this beautiful man who saved me—who knew how to tuck me in perfectly—who purrs at a frequency that I couldn't emulate from memory alone—I can't let him leave.

Something clicks in my mind: an elegant solution that satisfies both my inexplicable desire for Ace to stay and my analytical need for logical justification.

"You could stay," I blurt out, lurching toward him, hand outstretched.

His eyes widen with what I think may be hope. It causes a restriction in my throat and chest.

You're a scientist, not a lust-filled schoolgirl, Styles. Act like it.

I can't let him think I want him to stay for emotional reasons like lust or love. I recalibrate my posture, brushing invisible lint from my sweatshirt's front, and say with all the coolness I can muster, "For research purposes."

His face shifts to confusion, but his eyebrows raise in intrigue. "Research?"

I straighten and stiffen, removing all expression from my face and all emotion from my voice. "Yes, your presence has proven that the alphabots require significant improvements to their Care and Protection Protocols. Your natural alpha behaviors could provide valuable data."

"So, what? You want to plug me into a machine or something?"

"No, no," I say, shaking my head and moving closer to him. "They will observe you performing your natural alpha behaviors. Emulating you could significantly enhance their Heat Management Module."

Ace blinks, looking between me and the alphabots. "So you want me to...teach your robots how to be better alphas?"

"In short, yes. The data sources I've relied on to date have been... suboptimal. Introducing a live alpha that they can observe in real time materially increases the dataset's validity and quality."

"Where have you gotten your data so far?"

"Umm..." I blush, not wanting to tell him.

"You used pornos, didn't you?"

Heat rushes to my face. "And rom-coms!"

Ace chuckles and eyes the bots. One mimics Ace's chuckle and rubs the back of his neck, already picking up on some of Ace's mannerisms. Two smiles, then looks to the ground, simulating coyness. Three folds his arms and cocks his hip in feigned annoyance, as if waiting for Ace to initiate a dance battle—*which his programming supports, and I'd be down to see.*

Ace chuckles again at their reaction and says, "That makes sense."

He pauses for a moment, then asks, "Are you sure I'm the right alpha for this research, Cookie?"

"You demonstrated instinctive knowledge of nest arrangement that surpassed their programmed parameters. You can help them learn how to properly prioritize protection and care. Not to mention your natural purr has harmonics I haven't been able to replicate, and your scent modulation in response to my distress shows sophisticated pheromone control. Observing you perform your natural alpha behavior should provide extremely valuable data."

Ace scratches the back of his neck, a smile slowly spreading across his face. "So you want your bots to watch me and take notes on how real alphas act during an omega's heat?"

"Essentially, yes." I try to return to my professional tone despite the flutter in my stomach at his smile. I add quickly, "It will only be for a day or two."

There's a long pause between us.

Ace still doesn't agree to stay. He rubs the back of his neck again. He looks at his feet and kicks at the ground, considering my offer.

I'm terrified he's going to leave. I must make him stay.

Robots. He likes the robots. Maybe they can convince him.

I turn to Two. "Two, what's your assessment?"

"Based on current hormone levels, Beth's heat will likely resolve within 36 to 48 hours. Alpha-Ace's presence during this period would provide comprehensive data across multiple Care Phases," Two responds.

I nod, with an unrepressed, triumphant grin.

The perfect scientific justification.

Two continues to prove my point for me: "Alpha-Ace's rut state provides optimal conditions for studying protective and nurturing instincts. Precise observation of natural alpha behaviors would improve our mimicry capabilities by at least 42.8%."

I jump excitedly, letting myself get a bit carried away with the idea of studying Ace over the next two days. "See! The benefits would be significant, but with little effort from you."

I rush toward Ace and catch his hand, yanking him back from the door. "Documenting your instinctive responses to omega needs is just the beginning. I could record your purr to precisely model its frequency spectrum and modulation patterns. Deconstruct your scent at the molecular level to refine the bots' synthetic pheromones. Honestly—oh, wow—the volume of actionable data you represent is staggering."

Please stay.

I want you near me.

I feel safe with you.

The thought of you leaving makes my chest hurt in ways I don't understand.

Ace smiles at me, squeezes my hand, and leans down as if to kiss me. "So I'd just...what? Hang around here, be myself, and just let my rut do its thing?"

I try to contain the swell of excitement within me, but can't bring myself to drop his hand. "Within appropriate boundaries," I clarify quickly. "This is strictly for research. For science."

Ace smirks at me in a way that puts Three's carefully calibrated smirk to shame and asks, "For science?" The way he draws out the words suggests he can see right through my rational facade to the emotional truth beneath.

"Yes," I nod enthusiastically, my carefully constructed scientific justification momentarily forgotten, as I bounce on my toes.

10
ACE

I want nothing more than to say yes. The way she's excitedly pulling me back into her home, toward her nest, sends ripples of pure joy through me. I smile down at her, my cheeks aching with unbridled delight.

But the reality of what she's asking me to do hits me like a rogue wave, washing away my smile.

Stay here? With her? While she's in heat and I'm in rut?

She said, "Within appropriate boundaries." I'm pretty sure that translates to, "You can look, but you can't touch."

As much as I want to spend every single moment of the rest of my life with her...

I can't. I can't be near her for two days, unable to touch her.

My mind, my body...my heart—they can't take it.

I step back, rubbing my hand across the back of my neck. "I don't think that's a good idea, Cookie," I finally manage.

The unrestrained joy on her face drains as she drops my hand. But before her face fully smooths to careful neutrality, I catch a glimpse of vulnerability, disappointment, and sadness. If I weren't watching her so intently, I might have missed it entirely.

My heart bangs within my chest, trying to break out of my ribcage so it can kick me in the balls for making its girl sad.

"Of course," she says, returning her voice to that cold, scientific tone she used before she let herself get carried away. "That was presumptuous of me. The request was inappropriate."

She steps back, creating more distance between us. "Thank you again for your assistance. I'm sure you'd like to get away from me as soon as possible, considering our biological states." There's a slight tremor in her voice, cracking her scientific professionalism.

My heart breaks free of its confines and succeeds in its nut shot quest, screaming, "You fucking asshole, look what you did!"

She thinks I'm rejecting her!? This brilliant, beautiful woman thinks I don't want her.

"Hey," I say softly, taking a step toward her. "That's not what I meant."

She doesn't look at me; she just wraps her arms around her midsection and walks toward the stairs, saying, "Three, please escort our guest to the appropriate exit path. I'm sure he doesn't want to leave through the ocean. One, Two, accompany me to my nest while we await Three's return."

"Elizabeth," I try again.

"Dr. Styles," she corrects, still not meeting my eyes.

I rush to her side. I don't touch her, not yet, but I stand close enough that she has to look up to see my face. "Cookie," I say gently, "I'm not rejecting you."

Her brow furrows, but she still doesn't look me in the eye. "Your response pattern clearly indicates—"

"I want to stay," I interrupt. "More than anything. That's the problem."

She finally looks up at me and says, "I don't understand." She averts her eyes again, and I'm starting to realize eye contact makes her uncomfortable.

I take a deep breath, which is a mistake because it fills my lungs with her scent, and all the blood rushes from my brain to my dick. A purr rumbles from my chest, my body instinctively trying to comfort my omega's distress before my brain can even form the right words.

"I want to stay so badly that I'm scared of myself," I admit, the purr vibrating through my words. "I'm scared that if I'm around you for two more days, watching you move and hearing you talk about science stuff I don't understand...if I keep smelling your perfect scent and seeing how beautiful you are when you get excited about your robots..." I swallow hard. "I'm scared I won't be able to keep my hands to myself. And that's the last thing I want: to be another alpha who doesn't respect your boundaries. Which...I'm guessing is why you built these guys to begin with."

Her scent shifts subtly, the distress notes receding slightly. "Oh," she breathes.

Tentatively, I raise my hand, pausing to give her time to pull away before gently brushing a strand of hair back from her face. The electricity that runs through me when I graze her flesh is so intense, you'd think I was brushing a live wire off her cheek. My purr deepens at the contact.

She's so soft and warm, like a cookie right out of the oven. My teeth ache to take a bite from her, marking her as my omega forever. I don't bite her, but I do leave my hand against her cheek.

"If I could, I'd spend every moment of the rest of my life with you," I tell her, meaning every fucking word of it. "Not just these two days."

Elizabeth leans almost imperceptibly into my touch, her eyes wide and wondering. "Your purr," she says softly. "It's different from theirs."

"Because it's real," I answer simply. "Just like my rut is real. And the way I want you is real." I drop my hand reluctantly. "That's why it's dangerous for me to stay. I don't trust myself right now. My brain's not working right. I've never had a rut this strong before. I can't control it."

Because you're my omega. My scent-match. Can't you tell, too?

She looks back at me, and there's something new in her expression—a gleam of determination mingled with something softer, more vulnerable. "Your rejection of my offer is not due to some failure on my part," she states, not quite a question.

"No," I confirm. "The opposite. You're perfect. Your scent is making me rutting dumb...well, rutting dumber." I laugh, nervous and embarrassed, feeling inadequate in this moment—an unfamiliar feeling. Usually, I have no problem with my confidence. But this woman—this beautiful, perfect, brilliant woman—makes me feel like I don't deserve to be near her.

"My coconut scent," she says, and I'm surprised to see a tiny smile playing at the corners of her mouth, "is addling your already dumb brain? That is your assessment?" The smile turns into a full-blown devilish smirk, and I'm pretty sure that she's making a joke she finds deliciously funny.

I don't mind if she's poking fun at me, because that smirk is the most adorable thing I've ever seen. It bubbles an unrestrained laugh from my chest as my heart finally forgives me. "Yeah, that about sums it up."

"You're far from dumb, Ace," she says, and my name on her lips sends a shiver through me. "Your instincts demonstrated more intelligence regarding my condition than my extensively programmed alphabots."

I shrug, uncomfortable with the praise from someone whose IQ eclipses mine. "That's just basic alpha stuff. Nothing special."

"It is to me," she whispers. My heart flutters, moving past forgiveness and right into thanking me.

11
ACE

Something shifts in Elizabeth. Her pupils dilate engulfing her emerald irises, her cheeks flush pink beneath her pale skin, and her scent shifts, hitting me like a physical blow. The coconut-cookie sweetness intensifies, warming like sugar caramelizing, and beneath it comes something new—a rich, heady note of pure omega desire.

My knees actually buckle, and I have to catch myself on the edge of what I think is some kind of high-tech coffee table.

My rut, which I've been fighting to control since I first caught her coconut scent on the beach, roars to life with renewed intensity. My vision blurs white around the edges, funneling my sight on her, sharpening every detail of her face in crystal clarity—the slight part of her lips, the rapid pulse visible in her throat, the way her blonde hair falls across her flushed cheek. I know this means my pupils are overblown, clouded with the white haze of a rut.

Mine. Mine. Mine.

I recall her golden brown pubic hair, as her pussy wrapped around One's cock earlier today. *The same color as a coconut cookie.* My hand grips the edge of the table, stopping me from dropping to my knees and getting a taste of my cookie.

More blood rushes to my cock so fast my vision goes from white to black, and I sway.

Fuck. I might pass out.

"I need to—" I gesture vaguely toward the door, my brain struggling to form complete sentences. "Space. I need space, or I'm going to—"

"Your physiological response indicates extreme arousal," Two observes unnecessarily. "Rut pheromones increased by 163%."

"No shit," I stumble backward, trying to put distance between us.

"You want to fuck my omega, don't you?" Three asks with a smirk, his damaged face with a unicorn strapped to it adding to the ridiculousness of his asshole persona.

"You're not helping," I growl at the robots, backing up until my shoulders press flat against the wall opposite them. I place my hand over my sternum, holding my heart in place before it breaks free again.

Breathe, Ace. Get ahold of yourself.

The cool surface of the wall grounds me slightly, giving me something to focus on besides the overwhelming urge to cross the room and bury my face in Elizabeth's neck or pussy or anything.

Elizabeth watches me with those brilliant, analytical, green eyes. I can practically see her brain working, categorizing my reactions, forming hypotheses, as she collects data on her new research subject. But beneath that scientific assessment, there's something else—something warm and wanting that calls to everything alpha in me.

"You're maintaining distance," she observes, her voice slightly breathier than before. "Despite clear biological imperatives urging proximity."

I press my palms flat against the wall behind me, anchoring myself in place. "I'm trying, Cookie," I manage. "Your scent just got really...intense."

She takes a small step toward me, and I hold my breath.

"Fascinating," she murmurs. "The alphabots can detect the chemical changes but can't experience the corresponding urges." She glances at her robots, then back to me. "What exactly does my scent make you want to do, Ace?"

Bend you over that banister and make you scream my name.

Introduce you to my family.

Get on my knees and confess my love for you, then lick your pussy until you say, 'Oh, Ace, I'm never going to want a robo-tongue again.'

Hug you tight every night as I whisper how beautiful and brilliant you are.

Put a whole bus's worth of pups inside you.

Murder any motherfucker who so much as thinks a negative thing about you.

Plan our bonding ceremony. I'd like a cream-colored tux. You'd look beautiful in a pink so pale it's almost white.

Run outside and scream, 'I, Ace Beauvoir, found my scent-matched omega. Can you fucking believe it?'

"Things I shouldn't say out loud," I answer honestly. "Things I don't have the right to want."

She takes another step closer, her analytical expression softening into something more curious, more vulnerable. "But you do want them."

It's not a question, but I answer anyway. "Yes. God, yes."

Two nudges forward. "Caution recommended. Your heat cycle is still active."

Elizabeth holds up a hand, stopping the robot without looking away from me. "Would sexual activity without vaginal penetration and knotting be sufficient to address your rut needs?" she asks in a clinical tone.

I blink at her, certain I've misheard. "What?"

"Sexual activity without vaginal penetration," she repeats, those brilliant eyes fixed on my face. "Would that provide adequate relief for your current biological state?"

My brain short-circuits, struggling to process what she's suggesting.

Am I really one of her robots? Did she just run a magnet over my computer brain?

"Are you—" I swallow hard. "Are you offering to...with me?"

Three laughs menacingly as the unicorn bounces on his face. "Did she fucking stutter, alpha? I know alphas' cognitive functions decrease in proximity to omega pheromones, but this is pathetic. We're supposed to act like this guy?" he scoffs.

"Shut up, Three," Elizabeth says without looking at him, her attention focused entirely on me.

"I'm not on birth control," she explains. "Getting pregnant isn't something I want to entertain at this point in time—maybe never—but at least not for another five years. However, there are other activities that could provide mutual satisfaction while the alphabots and I study you. Specifically, there are penetrative activities that have a lower risk of pregnancy than vaginal penetration."

The matter-of-fact way she discusses this only makes it more surreal. My hands press harder against the wall, as if this wall is the only thing keeping me in this simulation I have obviously found myself in.

"You're asking if I want to...be with you. Sexually. But just not coming in you or knotting you." I'm fumbling for words, my usual straightforwardness failing me.

"Correct," she confirms. "Well, mostly correct. There are multiple non-procreative sexual activities that could address your rut symptoms while providing data for the alphabots' programming upgrades." She assesses my face, realizing I need it fully fucking spelled out for me, and says, "You may come in me and knot me, just not vaginally."

One steps forward to explain it to me, idiot to idiot: "The omega uterus can only be accessed via the vaginal canal. A knot ensures no semen escapes after ejaculation. But, now here's the fun part: semen knot-locked in any other orifice should not be able to reach the uterus. Thus, pregnancy is highly unlikely!" He holds up his finger as if he's explaining the secrets of the universe—*which, maybe he is...*

Elizabeth glances at One, annoyance crossing her face before she returns her gaze to me. "Your scent affects me as strongly as mine affects you." Her voice softens slightly. "I find that...surprising. And not unwelcome."

Not unwelcome? Does that mean 'welcome'?

I stare at her. This brilliant, beautiful woman can discuss sex like a science project while her cheeks flush pink and her scent calls to every primal desire within me. But she can't tell me exactly what she wants. And I think...I think she's saying she wants me.

The contrast between her analytical mind and her obvious physical response to me is more arousing than any fantasy I've ever had.

She could choose anyone. Fuck, she could build anyone. But it's me she wants.

"Say something," she prompts when I remain silent too long, a flicker of uncertainty crossing her features.

I push away from the wall, taking a cautious step toward her. "I'd be honored," I say, my voice rough with emotion and desire. "To touch you in any way you'll allow me to."

Her carefully constructed scientific facade slips for a moment, revealing something raw and vulnerable beneath. "Oh," she breathes.

"Not because of my rut," I continue, needing her to understand. "Not just because you smell incredible, or because I'm dying to know if you taste like coconut cookies everywhere." I take another step closer. "But because it's you. Because everything about you fascinates me. Your brilliant mind. The fact that you can build robots. The fact that you sleep in a pink nest hidden in this futuristic house."

She balks, unable to take these compliments. But her scent shifts again, the heated desire notes now mingling with something softer, sweeter.

"I'd be honored," I repeat, now close enough that I could touch her if I reached out. "But only if you're sure. Only if it's what you really want."

Elizabeth looks up at me, and for the first time since I've met her, she doesn't try to hide behind scientific terminology or clinical distance. "I want to know what it feels like," she admits quietly. "To be touched by a real alpha who looks at me the way you do. One who fights his own instincts to fuck me in order to protect me—to help me."

The vulnerability in her confession steals my breath.

I reach out slowly, giving her time to pull away, and gently brush the hair off her cheek again.

"I'll touch you however you want," I promise softly. "And stop the second you ask. No matter what."

She replies softly, "I believe you."

12
STYLES

I throw myself at him, my body moving before my brain can catch up. He catches me effortlessly, one strong arm wrapping around my waist.

This isn't like me—I don't do impulsive. I don't act without analysis, without weighing variables and calculating outcomes. But something about Ace's gentleness and earnestness shorts out my carefully wired self-control.

My arms wind around his neck. My chest presses against his. My hands tangle in his hair.

It's as if I'm drawn to him by some invisible force, and I pull his face down to mine before I can formulate a single coherent thought about the wisdom of kissing an alpha in rut.

The rational part of my brain drowns in the flood of omega biochemistry, sinking deep into its murky depths. His ocean scent envelops me completely, and for the first time in my life, I surrender to something I cannot control.

My mouth hovers over his as I study his face, watching his reactions.

"Cookie," he breathes, not closing the distance between our

mouths. Even now, trembling with the effort of restraint, he waits for explicit permission.

So I give it to him by pressing my lips to his. The contact sends electric currents racing through my nervous system, triggering a cascade of oxytocin and dopamine that makes my knees buckle.

I'm struck by how soft Ace's lips are: warm and pliant, moving against mine with a tenderness that makes something unfamiliar flutter in my chest. I've never understood the appeal of kissing. I always found it inefficient, messy, and an evolutionary relic designed to test genetic compatibility.

My alphabots can perform the mechanical action of kissing, but I never utilize it. Kissing serves no practical purpose during heat management. I added the functionality only for completeness—so that they could collect data on how useless it was and never do it again. Well, and perform it on each other to arouse me. But that too has never been necessary, as a) omegas don't need help producing lubrication during heat, and b) I don't have sex with them outside of my heat.

I thought I didn't enjoy kissing.

I was wrong.

Ace's mouth moves against mine with a gentleness that belies the strength of his powerful body and sends wave after wave of lust through me.

His hands come up to cradle my face, thumbs brushing my cheekbones with such delicate precision that I melt into him. When his tongue brushes against the seam of my lips, I open for him without hesitation, the action instinctive rather than calculated.

The taste of him floods my senses—salt and sunshine, like the ocean on a perfect summer day.

His purr vibrates through his chest into mine, the frequency sending delicious shivers across my sensitized skin.

"Cookie," he murmurs against my lips, and I feel rather than see his smile. "You taste even better than you smell."

I pull back just enough to see his face, his pupils blown wide with desire and rut, that ocean-blue nearly consumed by white, like the full moon that once shifted our ancestral wolves reflecting on the surface of the ocean. "You're the first person I've kissed in 5,362 days," I admit.

His thumb brushes my lower lip. "And?"

"I never thought I liked kissing," I confess. "It always seemed... unnecessary. Inefficient."

His smile widens, always making me wonder what its limits truly are. "And now?"

"Now I think..." I search for words precise enough to capture this new data point. "I think I may have had an insufficient sample size for my hypothesis."

He laughs, the sound rich and warm, vibrating through his chest and into mine. "Does that mean you'd like to do more research?"

Instead of answering, I press my lips to his again, relishing the soft groan that escapes him. Further evidence of his arousal presses hard against my stomach, and fresh slick gushes between my thighs in response.

His hands move from my face, sliding down my back to cup my ass, and before I can process the intention behind the movement, he lifts me effortlessly.

I wrap my legs around his waist instinctively, locking my ankles at the small of his back, gasping at the sudden, delicious pressure of his body against my clit.

"Nest," I manage to say between kisses. "Take me to my nest."

"Whatever you want, Cookie," he murmurs, already walking up the stairs, carrying me as if I weigh nothing.

My alphabots follow.

I'm unreasonably consumed by the sensation of Ace's hands supporting me, his fingers splayed across my ass, his thumbs pressing into the sensitive juncture where thigh meets hip. His touch burns through my thin cotton sleep pants, and I rock against him, seeking friction.

Sex with my bots has been clinical, scientific, just for a biological need.

But this—this is different. The need doesn't just resonate in my loins; it resonates somewhere else.

"Heart rate elevated to 112 BPM," Two announces. "Arousal pheromones increased by 157%. Temperature rising within acceptable parameters."

"Thanks for the play-by-play," Ace chuckles.

I should find Two's monitoring comforting. I designed him precisely for this function: to keep me informed of my body's condition at all times. Instead, I find myself annoyed by the intrusion, wanting nothing between me and the alpha carrying me up the stairs to my nest.

"Two," I command. "Observe only. No verbal updates unless Emergency Protocols are triggered."

Two nods, attempting to form a contrite expression. "Understood, Beth."

When we reach my nesting chamber, its pink softness envelops us. His eyes expand as he takes in the room. "I never realized how much I liked pink," he says as he steps forward.

He lays me down in the nest with a gentleness that makes my chest ache, as I sink into the familiar comfort of my space.

But as Ace lowers himself beside me, something sharp and panicked cuts through the heat haze. Reality crashes back into my consciousness. "Wait," I gasp, suddenly aware of what we're doing, where this is heading. My hand presses against his chest, holding him at bay.

Ace stills immediately, his hands leaving my body, creating space between us, and washing my body in a cold loneliness.

What am I doing? I can't have sex with an alpha I just met. While I'm in heat! Without protection!

I don't even know what he does for work. I don't even know his last name.

Pregnancy. A child.

My research disrupted. My carefully structured life altered beyond recognition.

My analytical mind kicks into overdrive, calculating probabilities, evaluating risks.

I try to elaborate on my worries. "I'm not on birth control. I never needed it with the alphabots."

Ace focuses on my face. "I know," he says gently. "You mentioned that earlier."

My heart races, matching my mind; my mouth attempts to keep up: "Even without knotting or ejaculation, there's still a chance of pregnancy from pre-ejaculatory fluid. Maybe we could get one of those condoms betas use, but that would only help with the pre-ejaculation fluid. If you knot-locked me and ejaculated, it would be rendered useless. I could take Plan B afterward, but the efficacy is reduced due to heat fertility, and—"

"Cookie," he interrupts, his voice soft but firm. "Look at me."

I do, finding his eyes clear and focused despite the rut I know is raging through his system. I do my best to maintain eye contact.

"I promised you," he says, his voice low and serious. "I won't. I meant it."

"But if you—"

"I won't put anything inside you that could get you pregnant," he says, each word deliberate. "Not my knot, not my cock, not even my fingers if they've been anywhere near my cock. Don't worry." He reaches out, slowly, telegraphing his movement, and tucks a strand of hair behind my ear.

"Besides," he adds with a grin that's both boyish and predatory. "I'm just gonna taste."

Heat floods my cheeks, but I don't look away. "Wait...what?" I trail off as he raises an eyebrow, his smile widening.

"I've been dying to eat some coconut cookies all day," he says, his voice dropping to a register that sends shivers down my spine.

13
STYLES

He sinks down my body. I watch, mesmerized, as he looks up at me with those ocean eyes. Waiting—asking permission without words.

I nod, unable to find my voice, and he smiles again—a flash of satisfaction that makes my heart stutter.

His fingers roam up my legs. His touch is nothing like my alphabots'. Where they are precise and efficient, Ace is intuitive and responsive, reading my body's signals in ways I never programmed into their algorithms. When he hits the spot behind my knee—the ticklish spot I've instructed the bots to avoid—I gasp and my core clenches. By the time his thumbs trace my inner thigh, my legs are trembling, and my arousal is overflowing.

He hooks his fingers in the waistband of my soft pants, strokes the skin on my abdomen, and asks, "May I?"

I breathe, "Yes," lifting my hips.

In one smooth motion, he tugs down my pants and panties. When the cool air hits my exposed pussy, I clench my eyes closed, gasping yet again.

Then his warm breath against my knee says, "Beautiful. So beautiful, Cookie." I open my eyes to see him staring at my exposed sex with reverence and wonder.

I should feel vulnerable. I've hidden in my home, rarely even turning on my camera for work meetings. Yet here I am, fully bare in front of this man, and I feel safe.

When he lowers his head, his breath is so warm against my center, I have to grip a pillow to keep from...*I don't know. Falling? That doesn't make any sense. I'm lying down. How could I fall?*

Then he does it!

The first touch of his tongue against my clit fractures my world into pure sensation. A sound pulls from my throat I've never heard myself make before: half gasp, half moan, wholly uninhibited.

"Mmm," he hums against me, and the vibration sends sparks up my spine. "Better than cookies."

I press the pillow I'm gripping into my face. Blocking the light. Blocking sound.

Too much input!

It's too much. It's too amazing.

Oral stimulation was the first sequence I perfected with my alphabots. We performed hundreds of controlled experiments to get their actions just right. Well, what I thought was just right. This is... better.

And I can't figure out why!

It is fundamentally, qualitatively different in ways I can't categorize.

The alphabots are predictable, but Ace is curious.

They follow patterns, but he explores.

It's chaotic.

It's erratically erotic.

I shouldn't like it...But I do. I fucking love it.

His tongue moves with an unpredictability that keeps me teetering on the edge. With each unexpected flick, a new spark of pleasure ignites within me.

"Oh God," I wail, losing my pillow and finding his hair. "What are you...what are you doing?"

"Savoring my meal, Cookie," he murmurs, then releases a satisfied hum against my clit, circling it with a gentle pressure of his tongue. Waves of pleasure radiate from our point of contact, curling my toes.

His purr deepens, just as he curls two fingers into me. My body arches forward. My hips rock against his mouth. I'm wailing out in pleasure.

But Ace doesn't stop, he doesn't slow, fuck, he doesn't even maintain the pace. He picks up his pace, and slides his free hand to my lower abdomen, holding me in place. The pressure inside me intensifies.

My fingers tangle into his hair, holding him in place, too.

He looks up at me—coming entirely undone—and I can see the smirk through his eyes—as pleased with himself as I am.

"Oh, fuck. Oh, God. Ace. Ace. Ace. Please don't stop," I plead, though I don't think it's necessary.

The orgasm strikes, overwhelming in its force, shocking me like a tidal wave. I cry out, my whole body shudders, and my core clenches hard around his fingers. The surge of pleasure arches my back and lifts me again. Ace's beautiful face is still between my thighs, not letting up, riding out the wave of my orgasm like it were the wave he rode in on. And just as he pumped that board and caressed that wave, he pumps and caresses me, guiding me through aftershocks of unrelenting orgasmic waves.

He pulls back only when I tug gently at his hair, needing his chest, his body, against mine. "Come here," I whisper.

He looks up, face glistening with evidence of my pleasure, and lets me pull him into a deep kiss, while wrapping me in a tight hug. I taste myself on his lips—coconut and something wilder. His body presses against my thigh, dick hard and still sheathed within sweatpants as he kisses my face, my neck, my chest.

I need it. I need to see it. My heat demands it.

I reach for it, pressing my hand against his hard length through the thin fabric. He breaks from his kisses, just long enough to inhale a deep, hissing moan. His eyes meet mine. I get lost at sea in the sparkling blue of his eyes and the salty essence of his scent.

Oooh. I bet his cock is as pretty as he is.

I tug the fabric down, freeing him.

When his cock springs free, I pause, taking in the sight of him. It's so perfect I could cry.

He's beautiful. Thick and hard and flushed and perfect.

Real.

And at the base, the beginning of his knot—already swelling with his rut, promising the fullness my body craves.

Mine.

"Ace," I gasp into his neck, as my teeth scrape against his flesh, wanting to bite him—wanting to consume him with my whole body. I reach for his cock, needing to touch, to taste, to experience this alpha who has turned all my careful calculations upside down. I wrap my hand around his shaft, and he groans, the sound so much more visceral, more real than anything my alphabots can produce.

When my fingers circle his knot, his whole body jerks against me. The reaction is so authentic, so unfiltered, that it sends a fresh wave of slick gushing from me.

I need his knot locked inside me. Need it with a desperation that obliterates every other consideration.

You'll get pregnant, you idiot!

I don't care. I need his knot!

But your five-year plan doesn't—

Fuck plans! Let him fuck you! I need him locked inside me, stretching me, filling me, completing me.

"I need—" I stop myself from saying, "your knot," as frustrated tears prick at the corners of my eyes.

But I don't need to say it, Ace knows what I'm thinking. He asks, "You need a knot?"

I nod, biting my lip. I close my eyes and spread my legs, positioning myself so he can enter me, but, instead, he says, "Two, come here. She needs a knot."

Huh? Two? He's not going to just knot me?

I open my eyes. Blink. Confused.

Two has been standing about a foot away, monitoring the situation: learning Ace's movements and tracking my metrics. At Ace's request, he stands tall, almost defiant, and responds, "This unit does not take commands from unauthorized users."

One and Three flank Two. They've been observing as well, while processing the data Two sent them through his advanced monitoring. At Two's refusal, Three crosses his arms, smirking, as if backing up Two's noncompliance. One looks back and forth between Two and Ace, as if watching a drama unfold.

"For fuck's sake," Ace mutters, then looks at me. "Cookie, can you tell him what you need, please?"

I turn to Two and command, "Two, initiate Knotting Sequence 6."

Two tilts his head in confusion in a way that only One usually does. "Conditions for Knotting Sequence 6 have not been met. Current heat metrics indicate—"

"Alpha-2," I interrupt sharply, using his full-name to indicate my annoyance. "We are in an Experimental Phase. Normal constraints do not apply."

Two nods. "Of course, Beth," and approaches the nest, removing his clothing.

Three and One give each other the look that indicates they are conversing wirelessly, likely wondering how many of their own constraints will be overridden by this experimentation phase.

As Two crawls beside me, Ace positions himself to the other side of me, cradling my face in his hands and wiping the tears I didn't realize had pooled on my cheeks away with his thumbs.

Two's movements are precise, efficient—exactly as I programmed them to be. His knot expands at my entrance as Ace places forceful, passionate kisses on my jaw.

And, as Two's knot stretches inside me, filling the emptiness, Ace whispers sweetly, "You're so beautiful like this." But, as if he were the one perfectly timed to precise algorithmic efficiency, at the exact moment Two's knot locks within me, he adds with a smirk, "taking his knot in that tight pussy."

My mind breaks once again. I wrap my legs around Two's torso, wailing out and clawing his back, letting an orgasm so intense rock through me that Two gasps, "Oh, fuck," which...is not something I've ever programmed him to say.

14
STYLES

It's not enough. Two's knot is not enough.

My heat is waning. I am fully in control of my wits. A single knot should be sufficient to satisfy the need of my heat. The deep ache in my core is gone, but there's another ache deeper in me.

I turn to Ace, and he smiles at me, with those impossible ocean-blue eyes and that impossibly kind smile, and I still need him. He has awoken a deep yearning within me that I can't quite explain.

Why? Why do I want this alpha? This unpredictable, unquantifiable man? What makes him more appealing than my precisely engineered companions?

My alphabots are perfect. They're calibrated exactly to my specifications, programmed to satisfy my every need with scientific precision. Yet...one touch from Ace sends more sensation through my nervous system than I think I've felt cumulatively over the last decade.

It makes no fucking sense! It defies my careful calculations—contradicts years of data collection.

Perhaps my brain is just responding to the novelty of newness.

Yeah, that's it! My brain is just releasing more dopamine in response to the new stimuli. That makes sense.

That's logical.

That's measurable.

That's explicable.

Ace presses his lips against my forehead; it's so impossibly gentle, but it topples my carefully stacked tower of scientific justifications like a wrecking ball.

That's not it. It's not the novelty. It's something else. I know it; I just don't know what it is.

Something in his touch reaches past the heat, past my biology, something I can't recognize or define...something I suspect I've kept locked away for a long time.

"It's not enough," I rasp out, trying to voice my feelings. "I need you."

Ace smiles and nods, kissing my cheek. "Of course, whatever you need, Cookie." He shifts his attention to Two. "Two, can you roll onto your back?"

Two's eyes spin, and his face falls to a confused frown. "Error. Singular vaginal knotting with concurrent oral penetration would be optimal given this stage of Beth's heat cycle."

"Huh?" Ace asks.

Two clarifies: "When I am knotting Beth vaginally, Alpha-3 penetrating Beth's oral cavity while maintaining his 'smirking' expression has historically produced optimal satisfaction levels."

Three unfolds his arms and pulls his dick from his pants. "You want my dick, don't you, Moonbeam?"

Ace's lips quirk in amusement, and my face flushes in embarrassment.

Two looks at me, his face contorting as he calculates all the possible things he could say next. "Beth, during this experimental phase, when presented with such a predicament, what would you have me do? Should I follow the unauthorized user's commands even when they contradict optimal procedures?"

Ace looks at me with a similarly questioning expression as he too awaits my commands.

Shit. I need to grant Ace authorized user status.

The whole point of my bots is to maintain complete control during my heat, even when I lose control. To give someone control over them is to go against their entire purpose.

I don't want to do it, but...

This cannot work if he's constantly fighting against their protocols. He needs to be able to act unfettered. My programming is obviously not optimal, and the bots need to be freed from the confines of my obviously insufficiently defined parameters.

This is for research.

For data collection.

For improving their algorithms.

"Alphabots," I say, "recognize Alpha-Ace as an authorized user."

A strange tingling thrill rips through my body. *Perhaps the dopamine of danger? No, it's just my omega biology responding to the idea of submitting to the authority of an alpha. Nothing more.*

Ace grins with boyish delight. "So I'm, like, the Prime Alphabot now? Leader of the robot pack?"

I chuckle. "Yeah. Basically."

One perks up. "Acknowledged. Alpha-Ace designated as Prime Alphabot. This unit will comply with Alpha-Ace's commands."

Two's eyes spin. "Requesting pack hierarchy clarification. Does Alpha-Ace usurping my position as Prime Alphabot indicate I am no longer to command Alpha-2 and Alpha-3 concerning procedures and sequences?"

I consider this for a moment. "You still have the authority and autonomy to make decisions concerning pack initiatives. However, Alpha-Ace's suggestions will take priority."

Three crosses his arms, the damaged synthetic skin of his face twitching slightly. "Do I still outrank Alpha-1, at least?"

"Yes," I reply, feeling a flicker of amusement at their power struggle.

One grins and nods at him. "I am now fourth! That is fun. Alpha-Ace is first. Alpha-2 is second. Alpha-3 is third. Alpha-1 is fourth. It is a modulo-three pattern!" He hugs the teddy bear against his chest and grins, releasing a stilted giggle, obviously pleased with himself.

Three nods, seemingly satisfied with this clarification. "Acknowledged. Pack hierarchy established."

"Alphabots, this arrangement is temporary and for research purposes only," I say more for my own sake than theirs. "Follow Alpha-Ace's suggestions and collect data on their effectiveness."

"Understood," Two confirms, shifting his weight above me.

Ace grins as wide as I've ever seen him and says with a chuckle, "Alright, now that that's settled. Listen up, brobots. Prime-Alpha-Ace is going to show you how a real alpha takes care of his omega. The kind of stuff they don't teach in porn and rom-coms."

'His omega'?

The words send a shiver down my spine.

It was a slip of the tongue. He meant 'their omega,' not 'his omega.'

I should correct him, establish boundaries, remind him that this is temporary—for research.

But...instead, I melt into the idea of being 'his'.

I can pretend...for just this heat cycle. What will that hurt?

Ace says, "Alright, Two, roll over onto your back, so that Beth is lying on top of you, okay?"

Two nods and wraps his arm around me to initiate the roll. But when Ace places his hand on my back to help Two roll me, a spike of panic cuts through me.

What will that hurt? It will hurt fucking everything!

What is wrong with me? What am I doing?

I can't give some random alpha I just met less than 24 hours ago authority over my alphabots!

My heat must not be as far along as I thought. It's heat head! I'm not thinking clearly, obviously!

I need to stop. I can't do this. I need to regain control.

"Wait," I gasp, gripping Two's shoulders and hugging him to me protectively. "Stop!"

Two squeezes me tighter, and Three stands at attention—both sensing something is wrong.

Ace senses it, too, and pulls away, removing his hand from my back. "Of course, Elizabeth," he says, and I note that he's using my real name. "We don't have to do anything you don't want to do. We can stop anytime you want."

His words should sound like empty alpha platitudes, something he says just to get his knot locked in me.

But...there's a sincerity in his voice that I can't quantify or analyze. There's a shift in his scent. There's a change in posture and facial expression. A million micro-cues that have a macro-effect. My rising panic ebbs, as if pulled by the gravity of his presence.

"You're in control here," he continues.

I look into his eyes, searching for deception, for the predatory glint I've learned to fear in alphas. I find only patience and desire tempered with concern.

I bite my lip, scared to reveal too much about myself, but I know I need to lay some boundaries down. "There is a list of things that are... ummm...hard stops for me."

He nods. "Like being restrained?"

I look down, dread flooding me. "Yeah, I...I..." I choke up, not sure how to explain. I try to continue, but my voice catches in my throat.

Ace nods again. "It's okay. You can tell me, Beth. I don't want to do anything you don't want."

"If you're going to...please don't..." *Why can't I say it? Why can't I tell him?* "Sorry, maybe this is...I don't know how to..."

He brushes a hair out of my eye. "Hey, they know, right? What was it called? Primary directions?" he asks, gesturing toward the alphabots.

I nod and I correct him: "Prime Directives."

He lifts to his knees and turns to Three. "Three. If I do anything against the Prime Directives, please give me one warning. If I do not stop within ten seconds, you can do that deadly force thing you've been itching to do."

"Understood, Prime Alpha," Three replies with a smirk, and crosses his arms to lean against the wall menacingly, despite the unicorn still attached to his face.

Ace turns to me. "Can he shoot eye lasers?"

I laugh. "No."

"Damn, you should add that. That would be super cool." He laughs.

Now I'm imagining Three shooting lasers from his eyes while surfing, and I have to admit, both would be super cool.

His smile melts, and he looks at me, his expression serious. "I can leave, Elizabeth. Just say the word. Do you want me to stay?"

I nod.

"I just want to make you feel good. To help you." He grabs my hand. "Do you want me to make you feel good, Elizabeth?"

I swallow hard and nod.

"Are you ready?"

I nod again.

"Can you say it for me, Cookie?"

"Yes. I am ready."

He kisses my cheek. "I got you."

I grin at him, melting into the idea of being 'his' again.

15
STYLES

"Two. Roll over. Slowly." Ace's voice remains calm, but now has a level of authority that makes my omega hindbrain gooey with arousal. "Keep your knot steady inside her. Don't hurt her."

Two complies. "Yes, Alpha-Prime."

I nuzzle into Two's neck, pressing close, as I wrap my arms around him.

Two grips my hip with one hand and supports my back with the other, as he turns. Ace guides the movement, his hand on my upper back while he supports my weight.

The roll shifts Alpha-2's knot, pressing it against my walls at a new angle that sends a fresh spark of pleasure up my spine.

When I gasp, Ace kisses my earlobe and whispers, "You like that, Cookie?"

Yes. And I like you kissing my earlobe.

Once Two is flat on his back, Ace kneels behind my upturned ass, gently rubbing my lower back in small circles, my hips rotate instinctively with his touch, rolling me around Two's knot as much as the lock will allow.

My slick readies me for Ace, and I can feel the rush through my whole body. I suck on Two's neck, nuzzling into him further, and marking him with my scent. Two eyes me, in what could be described as wearily, if he were programmed to do such a thing.

"Perfect," Ace murmurs, sliding his hand down my back, tracing the curve of my spine. He leans forward, presses his chest against my back to kiss my earlobe again, while whispering, "You look so beautiful like this, Cookie. So perfect taking his knot."

His warm breath and naughty, knotty words raise goosebumps along my neck. I shiver as his hands move to my hips, thumbs pressing into the dimples at the base of my spine.

"I'm going to fill you up," he whispers, dropping his voice to a register that makes my core clench even tighter around Two's knot—which seems impossible, but apparently it's not. "I'm going to stretch this pretty little ass while your toy fills your pussy. Would you like that? Both holes filled and stretched?"

The explicit words hit my body before they hit my mind. My mind is fast, whip-sharp usually, but I'm writhing, gushing, slick, and moaning before I can even process what he's said. And once I do process his words, I'm unable to form words of my own. But my body still works, so I can nod, at least.

I've programmed the alphabots to announce their actions before performing them. It helps me to relax if I know what's coming. But this...this isn't just to prepare...this is to arouse. *And boy, does it.*

"Good girl," Ace praises, and the simple phrase resonates through me like a physical touch. "I'll go slow. I'm going to savor every inch of you."

Honestly, if he keeps talking to me like this, I think I might lose a few IQ points from all the destruction and reconstruction my brain must do just to cohere his words.

He shifts to position himself behind me. With one hand on my hip, the other runs through my ass, gathering my abundant slick to prepare me. "Oh, Cookie, you're so wet for me."

He presses a finger into my ass, making me jerk; my nerves are on fire with anticipation. It doesn't hurt, but he strokes my lower back in small circles, calming me through it anyway. "Breathe, Cookie."

It's at this point that I know he's never been with an omega in heat, because this much tenderness and prep is unnecessary, but I'm enjoying it, so I keep my mouth shut and let him open my ass.

He moans as he presses forward. "Oh, fuck, Cookie. You're so tight. You're gonna feel so good wrapped around my cock."

I need to mark. I need to bite.

My teeth clamp down on Two's neck, sinking to the metal.

"Oh, you like that, Cookie? That's my good girl." Ace's finger slides inside, gentle but insistent, preparing me for more.

Two remains perfectly still beneath me, his knot a constant pressure inside me, but his eyes whirl as he processes my intense reactions with nothing short of bot-y bewilderment.

The dual sensation—Two's unmoving fullness and Ace's careful exploration—creates a counterpoint of pleasure that has me trembling.

Ace continues to work me open, adding a second finger, then a third, stretching me with careful attention while whispering a mixture of filth and sweetness in my ear. "So tight for me. Such a good girl, taking my fingers so well." Then, softer, "You're incredible, you know that? So beautiful. So brilliant."

By the time I feel the blunt head of his cock pressing against me, I'm a whimpering mess of desperation. I'm struggling to maintain coherent thought, the sensations overloading my nervous system, bringing all of my consciousness to the point where his cock finally connects with my body. Like a gravitational singularity, but instead of pulling all matter toward it, it's the only thing that matters.

"Ready for my cock, Cookie?" Ace asks, pressing a kiss to my shoulder blade, his member still notched at the entrance.

"Yes," I gasp, pushing back against him, seeking more. "Please, Ace."

He presses in, pleasure and pain fold into each other, my vision goes red, and spacetime collapses at the origin of our joining.

All thought wipes clean from my brain. My consciousness blips out.

And as he presses forward, each inch reconnects my neurons, stretching me, and rebuilding my brain.

I know there's a well-written analogy or funny joke around expansion, the big bang, him banging me, and naked singularities, floating somewhere in my brain. I know it's there. And I know it must be either really clever or really hilarious. But my mind still can't make coherent enough connections to form it, so I just giggle to myself, unrestrained.

He feeds his dick in, inch by inch, reconstructing me, grounding me back into a reality where time, space, and matter once again exist.

"Fuck, Cookie," he groans, his voice strained with the effort of restraint. "You feel amazing. So perfect."

My consciousness has returned, but my ability to form words and think coherently has not. I'm overwhelmed with the intensity of him and Two within me. I tremble, caught between them, filled to a perfectly unprecedented capacity.

Ace pauses once he's fully seated inside me, and he presses his chest against my back. His heart thrums against me, pulsing to the beat of Two's knot. He rests his chin on my shoulder, kissing my neck.

"Two, hold her tight for me. Not a restraint, a hug—light enough she can still move. Compliment her while kissing the top of her head. Keep that knot locked nice and tight in her, okay?"

"Understood, Alpha-Ace. Implementing Comforting Sequence 82," Two confirms, then wraps his hands around me and kisses the top of my head. "So beautiful, Beth."

Then Ace drags back his cock, sending a shock wave of pleasure so intense that I cry out.

I wrap my arms around Two's head, who kisses my neck and says, "That's our good girl," just like Ace had—he's learning quicker from Ace than I expected.

Ace establishes a rhythm—slow, deep thrusts that build in intensity, doing nothing to help me restore my brain's normal function.

"You want my knot, Cookie?" he asks, his voice rough with desire. "Want me to lock you up, fill you from both sides?"

"Yes," I manage, the word more breath than sound. "Knot me, Ace. Please."

He drives deeper, his pace quickening as his knot catches at my entrance with each thrust, swelling to the point of near locking.

The neurons he rebuilt for me earlier disintegrate again, and now I'm not even sure I remember what a neuron is.

I'm sinking into an ocean of sensation, surrounded by his scent—salt and sunshine and something wild that calls to the most primal part of me. It rushes in, washing away my carefully constructed walls. Ace is the tide, pulling me under, drowning me in pleasure.

"I've got you," Ace murmurs, his voice reaching me through the depths. "Ride the waves, Cookie. I won't let you drown."

Time becomes fluid, measured only by the rhythm of our breathing, heartbeats, and his thrusts.

Waves crash over me—orgasm after orgasm, each one stronger than the last, until I can't tell where one ends and another begins. I'm floating in warm waters, carried by currents of ecstasy.

I'm a babbling mess. Each thrust pushes a new phrase of nonsense out of me.

Thrust. "Oh, yes."

Thrust. "There, Two."

Thrust. "Poseidon's sea seed!"

Thrust. "Tidal forces!"

Thrust. "Spaghettification!"

Thrust. "There's the analogy!"

Thrust.

"That's it," Ace encourages, his rhythm never faltering. "Let go for me, Cookie. Stop thinking and just feel."

His words penetrate my fading consciousness, and something in me surrenders. Leaving me to my basest components of raw sensation and emotion.

For the first time in my life, I surrender completely to the moment—no calculations, no analysis, no attempt to control or understand—just pure, perfect sensation, washing over me like waves on the shore.

My mind drifts on cerulean tides, carried by currents of pleasure that ebb and flow with each pop of his knot within me. I float in this sea of satisfaction, anchored by the Two's knot, the press of Ace's weight on my back, and the deep thrust of his cock within me.

16
ACE

"Cookie," I groan, pressing my forehead between Elizabeth's shoulder blades instead of letting my teeth find her skin. "You feel so fucking perfect."

Her only response is a dreamy moan, her body limp with pleasure between me and the alphabot beneath her.

Two's eyes whirl. "This data is most extraordinary."

"That robo-speak for you're enjoying yourself, Two?" I ask with a laugh.

He looks at me like I'm clueless, *which...fair*.

"It means Styles is," Three grunts, sulking against the wall.

One is next to him, fidgeting with the robot equivalent of nervous energy. He's not quite pacing between Three and the nest; he's doing something that looks more like a kid trying to find the right time to jump into Double Dutch.

"One," I command, finding my voice deeper, rougher, more Alpha-Primey than usual. "Come here."

He responds, "Yes, Prime Alphabot," he says, leaping to my side over the invisible rope. I almost laugh at his dutifulness, but I gotta say, having power over these alphabots is extremely arousing. I know they're not real alphas, but being Prime Alpha of a pack is almost every little alpha's dream.

One stands, rigid like a soldier (or, ya know, a "person" made of metal), awaiting my command. The teddy bear strapped to his chest, and making his already cuddly chest look even more cuddly, stares at me as if to ask, "What depraved thing are you going to make us do?"

Just wait, Teddy, just wait.

I adjust my thrusts to a slower, deeper rhythm. Elizabeth whimpers beneath me, making me instinctively grip her hips tighter so I can push even deeper.

Gotta give my omega what she wants.

"Position yourself at her head. She needs something to suck," I tell One, but my eyes are locked on the point where my cock connects to Elizabeth.

Fuck, she's beautiful.

"I should activate a Face Fucking Sequence?" he asks, returning my attention to his tilted head and beautifully vacant face.

"Um, yeah," I confirm, stifling a chuckle. *A brilliant woman who writes code with things called "Face Fucking Sequence." God, I love her.*

"I have 132 Face Fucking Sequences. Should I perform all of them?"

"I dunno. Just pick one, bro. Just go kneel in front of her, dick out. She'll do the rest," I respond with slight annoyance. Now I think I know how Forrest must feel when he tries to explain his recycling system to me.

He nods, removes his pants, and clambers into the nest to kneel in front of Elizabeth.

She is lost in her heat now. When One positions in front of her, her eyes flutter open. They're beautiful, unfocused, hungry.

He looks to me for further guidance.

I tell him, "Let her take you in her mouth."

"Okey-dokey," he says with a dorky smile while his cock extends, inflates, and rotates slightly, changing shape.

Whoa! Cool! How does that thing work!? Is it, like, inside his gut and then extends out? I need to get my hands on that thing the first chance I get.

When his dick reaches her lips, she opens her mouth to him without hesitation. It's so fucking hot. My cock pulses, and Two's knot presses against me through her thin walls. I grip her hips and clench my thighs, using all my willpower to suppress my rut's desire, lock my knot in her, blow my load, and clamp my teeth down on her while reaching out and seeing what One's cock feels like.

I can't yet. I need the entire pack in on this.

I don't know why, but the moment they declared me a part of their pack, something unlocked inside me—an affection, a sense of brotherhood, a need to include and mentor. And as much as I try, I can't convince the alpha part of myself that it's not real.

Three's now standing at the door like a bouncer—legs wide and arms crossed, scowling like always, but the unicorn on his face vastly undermines the intimidation.

I point to the portion of the wall closest to the nest, behind One. "Three, lean against the wall there."

He complies—without any sass, which is surprising—and leans against the wall with a calculated casualness that projects aloof confidence.

"Stroke yourself," I command.

He removes his minimal clothing and releases his impressive cock. Unfortunately, his hand covers it before I can get a good look, but I think it works differently than One's, and I swear I saw it rotate.

I return my attention to Beth's behind and close my eyes, ready to lock, but...

Something's not quite right. The vibe is off...

Yeah, I could finish now, but I need my first time with my pack to be perfect—not just for her, but for all of us.

Focus, Ace. What's missing?

I scan the room, trying to find what's missing, and I wish I had Two's eyes right now. The saturation of my and Elizabeth's pheromones envelops me in a warmth that just feels like fate—it's like sitting on the beach on a warm summer day while enjoying warm coconut cookies—with the added bonus of fucking the love of your life in the ass.

Oh, that's it. It's just the two of us.

"Alphabots, increase your pheromones. And before you ask about percentages or whatever, just make your best judgment," I command, adjusting my angle to hit deeper inside Elizabeth and making her moan around One's cock.

The bots comply, each adding a slight variation of French vanilla coffee to the mix. Now it's a cool summer morning, and I'm sitting on the beach, fucking my girl in the ass, while doing a crossword puzzle, sipping a cup of coffee, and eating coconut cookies.

I wonder if their bottiness is what adds that crossword-puzzle undertone?

The vibe is still not quite right. Three...

"Hey, Three, continue to look aloof—too cool for all this. Keep that whole bad-boy thing you're doing up, but adjust your pheromones to signal deep love. Can you do that?"

Three's eyes spin and go red for a split second.

Did I accidentally tell him to kill me?

I gulp.

He responds, "I have the chemical compounds necessary to create pheromones that meet your request. But clarification is required. Bad Boy Protocol limits my emotional pheromone output to maintain character integrity. Are you requesting I rewrite the parameters of Bad Boy Protocol?"

Uh...am I?

"Umm...Two?" I ask, still thrusting into Elizabeth, but leaning around to get a better look at his face.

Two understands my confusion and says, "Alpha-3, all commands during the Experimental Phase should be treated as temporary overrides and not full overwrites until analysis on effectiveness can be accurately measured."

Three asks me, not Two, "Prime Alpha, does your request imply we are re-prioritizing the mental components of omega arousal and not just focusing on the mechanical actions of physical stimulation?"

Uh...what?

I look to Two for help. He answers, "Affirmative."

Three nods. "Good. I never agreed with that deprioritization." His smirk is a close approximation to a smile—I'm not sure if his face can do anything other than a one-sided smirk, actually. Then, something in his expression shifts, and I swear I see a moment of genuine emotion pass across his face. The air shifts subtly—less aggressive, more adoring.

Elizabeth responds immediately. She tenses between me and Two, and moans in delight around One's cock. Her scent sweetens further, the coconut notes blooming with vanilla warmth.

This is so surreal. I'm having an orgy with a pack of robots!

The absurdity of it hits me in a wave that breaks through my rut-haze and stutters my movements. I never imagined my day would lead here: commanding a trio of robots while buried deep inside the most fascinating woman I've ever met.

I wasn't even planning on surfing this morning. I was on my way to the airport—on my way home. But something about the way the sun glinted off the waves convinced me I had time to get one last surf in before my flight.

Ha, I guess I missed that flight. I bet my rental car's been towed by now. Fuck. Oh, well. I'll deal with all that later.

I should probably call Tom and Forrest and tell them I won't be home...

Elizabeth rocks between me and my robo-packmates with increased urgency, and I can't worry about the mess I've probably made of my life right now. I need to please my omega. Nothing else matters.

I speed my rhythm, matching hers. One picks up on it as well, tangling his hand in her hair and guiding her head onto his cock with new speed.

Elizabeth whimpers, her orgasm desperately trying to claw its way out of her, and she tenses under me.

I purr, and she relaxes as I drive deeper into her. Two, uninstructed, purrs, as well. The sound vacillates and shifts until it harmonizes with my natural rumble. One and Three follow suit.

She's so close. I can tell by the way she pushes back against me. I can tell by the desperate sounds she's making around One's cock. But most of all, I can tell by the way her coconut scent is wrapping around me, filling my lungs, penetrating me as I penetrate her.

I'm gonna make my omega come so hard she'll never look at another dick, real or robotic, without thinking, 'This is a nice cock, but shucks, I wish it was Ace's.'

My Mate. My Mate.

Mine. Mine.

The words echo through me, dangerous and enticing. My knot grows more, catching at her rim with each thrust, egged on by my fantasies of claiming her.

I press my face into her hair, breathing in the coconut sweetness of her as my rhythm falters, overcome by sensation. The urge to sink my teeth into her neck grows stronger, an almost physical pain to resist.

She's not my mate. Not yet.

Maybe never. Probably never.

I'm just a data point to her...a monkey she sends off to space to see how long I take to die of radiation...

But my body doesn't understand the difference, especially not with her scent filling my lungs and her tight heat gripping my cock.

"Mine," I whisper, too quietly for her to hear over her own moans and the mechanical hum of her alphabots.

The pressure builds at the base of my cock, radiating into my core. My knot is so swollen it's almost painful. Every pop past her rim feels like it will be the locking thrust into Elizabeth's perfect little ass.

I'm close. I don't have much left in me, but I'm determined to make her come at least one more time before I lock inside her, rendering myself relatively useless for twenty minutes.

She just needs something: one final push to send her over the edge.

"Three," I call out, while rubbing small circles at the base of Beth's spine. "Come closer."

Three pushes off the wall, and approaches the nest, still stroking his cock, which I think might be ribbed.

Fuck, that's hot.

Elizabeth has good taste and designed these bots to be physically perfect. It takes a significant amount of mental energy to convince my brain they're not actual humans. My body, however, is harder to convince, and I need to bite my lip and avert my eyes so the sight of him doesn't make me finish too early.

Eyes closed, I say, "I'm going to lock inside her. When I do that, you come onto her back. Time it perfectly."

He says, "I'm going to paint your back, Moonbeam."

I dare to open my eyes and look at One, who's still feeding his cock into Elizabeth's eager mouth. "One, come in her mouth at the same moment. Synchronized."

One simply grunts and nods.

I close my eyes again and nearly lose myself to the sensations of Elizabeth sliding over my knot, but I compose myself and say, "Two, restart your knotting sequence to sync with mine, okay?"

Two replies, "Yes, Alpha-Prime," and a boy could get used to this level of obedience from his packmates.

Three kneels at Beth's side, between me and One, and I'm finally able to get a good look at his cock. It's definitely ribbed, and it is definitely spinning as his hand pumps up and down it.

Three notices me looking at his cock. He smirks, like always, and says, "Like what you see, Alpha-Ace?"

My thrusts falter slightly, taken aback by the challenge and, honestly, embarrassed that he's called me out on ogling him. "Oh, yeah, uh, sorry for staring. I am just...really fascinated by robots."

Three's smirk deepens, and he says, "Let me know if you'd like a closer look sometime."

Is he hitting on me?

Before I can respond, he presses a kiss to the side of One's neck.

Elizabeth's eyes widen, and a high, needy whine vibrates through her whole body and right up my cock.

Three whispers something in One's ear, then returns his gaze to me. One detangles one of his hands from Beth's hair and then wraps it around Three's cock.

Three says, "She likes it when we fuck each other. Now that we're re-prioritizing the mental components of her arousal, I can teach you all about it, Prime Alpha."

Okay, yeah, he was hitting on me.

She likes it. Really likes it. Her reaction is immediate and powerful. She hums, once again, but this time it is so loud that it visibly vibrates the sparkly, thick-with-pheromones air around her.

Three tilts his head back and lets out a contented sigh, "This is what I was built for: the mental component."

One looks down at Elizabeth and says, "Sunshine has always liked it when I assist Alpha-3 with his Ejaculation Sequences."

Three growls, "That's because you're so fucking good at it, Alpha-1." He returns his mouth to One's neck and kisses him, running his hand down One's side, avoiding the teddy bear, and then weaving his hand in Beth's hair along with One's. Together, they guide her head along One's cock.

Elizabeth bucks more violently against me.

I reach around her, finding her clit where Two's cock stretches her, and that was the last thing she needed; she's wailing out, orgasm crashing over her, clenching around my cock and squeezing Two's knot so tightly with mine that I lock in place.

And it's not just her finishing. The feel of her hard, slick bud and Two's smooth cock sliding so erotically against my fingers, the tightness of her heat around my knot, the sight of Three and One together...*I'm done.*

I press my lips close to her ear. "Ready for my sea seed, Cookie?"

She says what sounds like yes, despite the cock down her throat.

"I'm coming," I rasp out, just as my knot expands, blurring my vision. "Now. All of you. Now."

The response is immediate and synchronized with such precision, I'm once again wondering if I'm one of her robots, too, and all my memories are false.

Three groans, and his cock pulses within One's grip. And as the first hot wave of my release pulses within her, his shoots onto her back, coating it with synthetic seminal fluid.

One's body tenses as he empties into Elizabeth's mouth.

Two announces, "Initiating Synthetic Ejaculation Sequence and resetting Knot Timer," from beneath her. His knot swells and pulses against the thin walls of her, massaging my knot, as he pumps his load into her.

And me, well, I nearly black out as my release dumps deep inside her, seeking a womb it won't find. The pleasure is so intense it's almost pain, radiating from the base of my spine outward in waves that make my entire body shake.

But Elizabeth's reaction surpasses all of ours.

Her body convulses, caught in an orgasm so powerful that she screams around One's cock, the sound muffled but unmistakable. Her scent explodes into the room—coconut and vanilla and omega satisfaction so complete I can't help but purr with pride.

Then, as quickly as the storm hit, she goes completely limp between us.

For a moment, I panic, thinking something's wrong—until Two's calm voice cuts through my concern. "Beth has entered unconsciousness due to pleasure overload. Vitals stable."

I, too, am about to lose consciousness. I lean forward, resting on Elizabeth's back slightly but carefully not to put my entire weight on her.

Three places a pillow at Elizabeth's side and points at it for me.

"Thanks," I say.

He nods and grunts in return.

My knot tugs just slightly, not enough to hurt, but enough to remind me to move slowly, as I lie on the pillow, closing my eyes.

"Alpha-Prime," Two whispers, and I open my eyes to look into his face near mine. "Thank you for your assistance. The data collected during this session has been invaluable for future programming improvements."

"Glad I could help," I murmur as I let myself drift to sleep in the embrace of my pack.

17
STYLES

I peel a strip of silver duct tape from Two's damaged leg and toss it to the mangled pile of multicolored tape discarded on my laboratory floor. "I think I've removed an entire roll of duct tape just from Two's leg," I say to Ace.

Ace stands beside me—actually, stands isn't quite right...

Ace fidgets, taps, and touches everything as he hovers beside me and watches me repair the bots, who lie on worktables in various states of disassembly.

He ceases his irregularly rhythmed tapping on the tabletop beside One's head, and peers at Two's leg over my shoulder. His breath tickles my neck, sending an involuntary shiver down my spine. It's pleasant but somehow also too much, like eating 168 cupcakes in one sitting.

"I might've gotten a bit carried away," Ace replies. His chest presses briefly against my back, a casual touch that sends another shiver through me.

He hasn't been still since we entered the lab, as if his body physically can't contain the energy coursing through it. And he keeps touching me casually like this.

I try to focus on the delicate repair work rather than the beautiful alpha who keeps finding excuses to brush against me. But even when he's not touching me, I can feel him dithering behind me, washing his ocean scent over me in distracting waves.

I need to finish these repairs and get some work done before my next heat wave hits. The lucid periods between flares are precious time I can't afford to waste, but it's impossible not to engage with him —impossible to ignore him.

His energy is...a lot. The laboratory feels too small, too warm, too full of sound and movement, and ocean scent.

I tug at an especially stubborn piece of tape holding Two's synthetic skin to the linear actuator in his leg, and mumble, "Carried away is an understatement."

Ace laughs, a full, unguarded laugh. "Hey, I was working with limited resources. Plus, it's not like they teach sex robot repair in school."

"It is remarkable that it was sufficient to override their Structural Integrity Protocols," I say as I carefully remove the flesh panel from Two's legs, fully exposing the metal sheathing underneath. I'm hyper-aware of Ace's eyes upon me—as if I'm the one whose flesh has been removed, hidden components exposed.

I adorn my magnifying loupes and switch on their light, illuminating Two's leg.

Ace grins, that disarming smile that makes something flutter in my stomach. "I just kept adding tape until they said they were fixed enough to be cuddleable."

I fumble with my microdriver. Each micro-movement Ace makes causes a different muscle within me to tense. I've dropped so many tiny screws at this point that I now have a jar of replacements next to me.

"Yes, well," I clear my throat, "your improvisation skills are commendable, if unconventional. Your repair techniques are..." I search for a diplomatic word as I scrutinize the tangle of adhesive, "creative." I reach for my soldering iron and take a deep breath, so that I can perform the delicate work.

"You can say it's a disaster. I've never claimed to be a robotics genius." Ace briefly touches the small of my back as he gapes over my shoulder at Two's exposed circuitry, now illuminated by my loops.

The casual contact startles me. The soldering iron wavers slightly in my hand, and I set it down before I can damage something. I'm not accustomed to being touched so freely, so easily. The alphabots only touch me when necessary or directed—their movements predictable, programmed.

What is wrong with me? I want Ace to be near me, but I also want him to go away.

I don't have the language for this contradictory feeling.

"Disaster is perhaps too strong," I say, disconnecting Two's damaged knee joint motor and placing it aside before lifting my loupes to my forehead and rolling my chair to inspect Three.

I snort, unable to contain my amusement as I examine the unicorn plushie still partially attached to Three's face. "And this? Was this structurally necessary, or just aesthetically pleasing?" I ask, pointing at Three.

"Structural integrity, obviously," Ace says with mock seriousness.

I chuckle. "Yes, I see. And the teddy bear?" I ask, pointing at the teddy bear attached to One's chest.

"Very advanced engineering techniques. You wouldn't understand," Ace replies, and I can hear the smile in his voice without looking at him.

This shocks a genuine belly laugh from me. "Oh, really? Elucidate me, oh wise robot repairman."

"Three's jaw was kind of jutting out at this hard edge. I didn't want you to cut yourself on his face, so I thought the unicorn would soften the edge. One's chest was caved in. I assumed you made his chest so beefy because you liked cuddling it, so I thought the teddy would be a good replacement." He winks and places his hand on the back of my chair, grazing my back with his thumb.

The touch sends a ripple of awareness through my skin. His proximity makes my heart rate increase—an involuntary physiological response I'm still not entirely comfortable with. I shift slightly, creating space between us and focus intently on removing the unicorn from Three's face, not trusting myself to look at Ace or to do anything that involves a soldering iron or tiny screws.

Once again, my heart races as I struggle with the best way to respond. I can't lie and say he did a good job, because he most assuredly did not. But I can't deny that the results, while not optimal, were sufficient, and I am compelled to acknowledge his effort.

But, if I don't blindly praise him, he'll get mad at me...just like everyone does. I say a fact, they hear an insult, unless I put a spin on it. And my brain wasn't designed to apply conversational torque. I try anyway, "Your methods might have been unconventional, but they proved to be effective."

Was that rude? I can't tell.

I clear my throat and add, "Thank you. For repairing them enough that they could help me." I avoid eye contact just in case that wasn't a sufficient amount of gratitude.

"You needed them, Cookie. I did what I had to do." The lighthearted teasing is no longer present in his voice. Its sincerity, paired with his use of that ridiculous nickname, catches me off guard. A disorienting warmth unfurls in my chest.

Ace turns to me, grins, amplifying the unfurling warmth, then quips, "Plus, One looked jealous of Three's unicorn. Couldn't have that."

I laugh, but make sure I throttle it so I don't embarrass myself. "I'm sure he did," I reply, knowing full well One does not have the capacity to express jealousy.

Ace's expression turns apologetic, serious again, and he says with genuine concern in his voice, "Sorry again about wrecking your guys," while absently stroking my hair back from my face and tucking it behind my ear.

I freeze, unsure how to respond to the gesture's casual intimacy. My skin tingles where his fingers brushed my cheek. And his constantly shifting tone and facial expressions are giving me communication whiplash—the moment I think I have settled into a comfortable rhythm with him, he changes tactics.

I hate this. This feeling of inferiority I only ever feel when locked in small talk with someone who vastly outranks me in the sociability department. It's so easy for him, but it takes a lot of mental effort from me.

Maybe he actually likes me. Me. Not the me everyone makes me pretend to be. Maybe I don't have to try so hard with him.

No, he won't. No one ever does.

After what is likely too much time to be considered neurotypical, I finally say, "They'll be fine." I roll away under the pretense of reaching for a tool and add, "The damage is repairable. Most of these components are modular and can simply be replaced. The most difficult part will be applying the skin panels. The seams can be a pain to line up."

The space allows me to breathe again, but Ace immediately follows, his body seemingly magnetically drawn to mine. "Can I help? I promise not to use any more duct tape or stuffed animals."

"I've got it," I say, more sharply than intended.

His face falls slightly, and I feel a pang of... something. Not quite guilt, not quite regret, just an awareness that I've disappointed him. *I wasn't trying to. I really do 'got it!'*

I modulate my tone and try again. "But thank you." I force the smile I've been told is attractive and friendly.

He returns my smile, and even as he smiles at me, I can tell that I'm mucking this whole thing up.

I'm not good at this—at people, at emotions, at navigating the complex terrain of human interaction without an algorithm to guide me. Usually, I limit my interactions with other humans to text. At the very most, I'll video chat, but even then, I have multiple monitors feeding me data on appropriate and possible responses. It's a lot like the stream of data Two receives on me.

I can't maintain this smile anymore, and I think I've crossed the threshold of how long to hold it before I look creepy.

I roll back to Three, so I can put both my and Three's faces back in their natural states. I start replacing Three's jaw, but Ace is once again at my side, literally breathing down my neck as I perform the delicate work.

I stiffen as his proximity sends another ripple of uncomfortable electricity through my skin. This level of intimacy is casual for him. I can tell by how he does it so effortlessly, so absentmindedly, but the feeling is so foreign to me it could be construed as...*invasive? Is that the feeling?*

My laboratory is my safe space, even safer than my nest. It's where I go when I need quiet, predictable solitude. But right now, it feels...loud, stifling, and crowded.

My lungs can't expand fully with him standing so close, and it's not just because his ocean scent fills every breath I take. The sense of eyes continuously upon me magnifies my awareness of every possible mistake I could make with even the slightest action.

"Am I distracting you?" he asks, noticing my slight flinch.

"No," I lie, then correct myself. "Yes. Maybe. I just—I need to concentrate."

"Sorry," he says, but instead of moving away, he places his hands on my shoulders, kneading gently. "You're tense. Let me help."

His fingers press into muscles I didn't realize were tight, and I have to bite back a hiss. It feels good—too good—and yet simultaneously makes me want to crawl out of my skin.

"Thanks," I manage, fighting the dual impulses to pull him close and push him away. I don't understand why I feel both simultaneously: why his presence is both comforting and suffocating.

All I know is that I need to focus on repairing my alphabots and getting back to my work while I'm still clear-headed enough to do it.

The rest—these confusing, contradictory feelings about the alpha who crashed into my life—will have to wait.

"I need to finish these repairs," I say quietly, shrugging his hands from my shoulders. "My heat will surge again soon, and I'll need them functional for it."

"You have me for that," Ace replies with a mischievous grin.

"Yes, but—" I stop, unsure how to explain that I need the predictable, programmable comfort of my alphabots alongside whatever this new, wild thing with Ace is.

How do I tell him that his constant presence, while not unwelcome, is simply...a lot?

I don't know how to articulate that I'm used to being alone, that other people's energy drains me in ways I can't quite quantify. That even someone I'm attracted to—someone whose touch sets off fireworks under my skin—can become overwhelming when there's no space to breathe.

One part of me is touched by his eagerness to help and that adoring look on his face right now. Another part feels smothered by his constant movement, his unpredictable touches, his very humanness.

It's not that I want him gone exactly, just...less.

Less touching, less movement, less scent, less sound.

It's like my sensory processing is overwhelmed, every input dialed to maximum intensity. Even the sound of his breathing feels amplified in the quiet lab.

"Ace," I say, not entirely sure what I'm going to follow it with.

"Yeah, Cookie?" He's beside me again, close enough that the heat radiates from his skin.

Before I can formulate what to say next, a flash of movement on my computer monitor catches my attention.

Neon green text scrolls across the display, within an uninvited pop-up window:

HELLO THERE, TORQUECAT!

I groan as a crude animation of a coffee cup with steam rising from it appears, and lines of code scroll rapidly, attempting to breach my system.

"What the hell is that?" Ace asks, leaning closer to peer at the screen.

"That," I say with more annoyance than concern, "is Percolate."

18
STYLES

"Percolate?" Ace asks.

I remove my magnifying loupes, and I roll my chair to my computer terminal, putting physical distance between myself and Ace. "A hacker who thinks he's my arch-nemesis."

"Should we be worried?" Ace asks, his body language shifting subtly toward protective mode—shoulders squaring, stance widening.

I can't help but smile at his concern. "No need for alpha heroics. He's harmless—more irritating than threatening. It's actually almost endearing how persistent he is, despite never succeeding."

The pop-up bounces around my screen like it owns the place. It's loud, performative, flashy—like everything Percolate does.

I sigh at how uninspired the whole thing is.

Code floods the display, emulating the visual style of a recent movie, all the dorks who posture as actual programmers are obsessed with.

I don't even bother disconnecting from the network; I just open a terminal window and type the commands that are muscle memory at this point. I've had to do this so many times that I can do it in my sleep.

The UI for my bespoke system monitor pops up, providing all the data I need to track the situation and respond if necessary.

I watch and wait.

Ace watches the numbers tick with evident fascination and clear cluelessness. "So you have an arch-nemesis?"

I roll my eyes and groan.

Ace adds, "That's kind of cool. You're like some superhero up here in your lab, fighting crime, building sex bots, looking hot."

"He's not my arch-nemesis!" I insist, amused at the look he's giving me, but determined to correct the fallacy. "I said he 'thinks he's my arch-nemesis.' He's just some annoying script kiddie who decided I was his arch rival years ago and sends me these little elementary school viruses once in a while."

"Still," Ace says with a grin, "it's pretty cool."

I break my gaze from the screen to inspect his face. He's looking at me in a way that threatens to flare my heat symptoms. Despite myself, I smile.

I return my gaze to the monitor: the only thing spiking is my heart.

An animation of a cat sipping coffee pops up. "What's that there?" Ace asks, pointing at it.

"Oh, that's just a visual for my countermeasures. It tells me his attack has been contained."

"So he's just some guy who randomly decided you're his nemesis?"

I shrug. "Basically."

"Why does he target you specifically?"

"No idea," I say, trying to remain nonchalant.

Ace looks at me incredulously, eyebrow raised.

I falter, breaking my gaze from the screen again to defend my lie more convincingly. "Seriously. I have no idea. I assume he's some alpha with a God complex, somehow spurred by some message board or something. Some interaction that meant nothing to me but everything to him."

He squints at me. "But, like, why you? Why would someone think you're arch-nemesis worthy? I know you're smart, but there's something you aren't telling me."

I grin. "Well, he thinks I'm some semi-anonymous alpha who looks like Three and goes by the name ToRQUueCaT—which is half-right, I guess."

"ToRQUueCaT? Why does that sound familiar?"

I sway my chair back and forth, pleased with myself. "My efforts have been documented by the news media occasionally." I blush at the ground.

"Wait...are you the hacker that wiped out all those student loans last year?"

"Yeah, that was me," I say.

"Oh, wow, you ARE like a superhero. You've got a secret identity and everything." He chuckles.

The cat animation morphs to a cat wearing a chef's hat and making biscuits.

"What's your counter-kitty-thingy doing now?" he asks.

I giggle. "That's my counterattack. He accessed my standing mixer for some reason. So, it's ensuring the next time he tries to look at porn on any device on his network, he'll be directed to a fascinating live stream of a sourdough starter."

"Malicious, Cookie," he says with a level of sarcasm even I can read.

"Well, you know. He started it," I respond with a huge grin.

The cat transforms into a cat dressed as a professor.

"What's the measuring kitty doing now?"

I'm fighting a smile now. "Usually I send him a code review, give him little hints about his flawed approach, and how he can do better next time."

"Wait? You give the guy attacking you tips on how to be better?"

"Well, yeah. Sometimes I feel bad for him and throw him a bone, but I don't have time for that right now."

I close the countermeasure window and turn to Ace.

"That's...surprisingly sweet of you," Ace says, looking at me with an expression I can't quite read.

"It's not sweet," I correct him. "It's mentoring. If he doesn't learn, he could do real damage—not to me, but to others."

"Sure, sure." He raises his hands in surrender. "Totally cold and calculating. Not sweet at all."

"Seriously, he does some reckless, high-profile stuff. If I don't help him, innocent people could get hurt by his idiocy."

"Hold on...Percolate...didn't he, like, expose that rideshare company that was stealing tips?"

"Yeah, like I said, 'script kiddie.'"

"Maybe I don't know what a script kiddie is, but...isn't he like the best hacker in the world?"

"SECOND FUCKING BEST! Getting caught doesn't make you good! The only reason he's well-known is because of how performative he is!"

"But, you took credit for that student loan thing," he smirks at me the way Three does. "That sounds pretty performative to me."

"Well...I only did that to...nevermind, I don't want to say."

"What?"

"Originally, that was his whole thing, but his code was so bad! He was taking a few cents off the loans every day. I think he thought the banks wouldn't notice. But they did! And people needed real help, like tens of thousands of dollars kind of help! A few scents per day wouldn't be enough to help people. So I just...fixed it for him. I took credit to teach him a lesson in humility."

Ace smiles so wide I can almost see his molars, and his scent spikes.

"What?" I ask.

"You're something else. You know that?"

"Oh, um...thank you, I guess," I say, my eyes darting to the ground, uncomfortable with the way he's not breaking eye contact and hovering over me.

He reaches out to touch me again, but I roll away, putting my magnifying loupes back on my head, and stopping near the table where One lies motionless. "I should get back to it..."

Ace is moving again, picking up tools and setting them down, touching the alphabots' exposed circuitry. He's pacing around the lab, his energy filling the room like a physical presence even more overwhelming than before—it's reminiscent of earlier today when he was pacing in the living room.

Did I do something wrong? Is it because I keep rolling away when he tries to touch me?

What does he want from me?

I carefully cut the teddy bear away from One's chest and try not to focus on the constant movement of Ace in my periphery.

Suddenly, he rushes to my side, as if some resolve has come over him. "Hey, can I uh, talk to you for a minute?"

"Um, I really should—"

"It'll be quick, I swear. I just...I've been trying to think of the best way to say this to you, but I can't think of a good way, so I just need to say it." Ace shifts uncomfortably, his scent changing subtly—the calm ocean gaining an undercurrent of something warmer, more nervous.

Here it comes. Here's where he tells me all the ways I need to change.

I should have known he was too good to be true. No one can be that perfect.

"Um...okay." My fingers go numb, and my hands freeze on the panel of synthetic skin I'm peeling back on One's chest plate. I raise my magnifying loupes to my forehead, and I sit on my hands to hide their trembling. I set my facial expression as still as I can.

Neutral. Calm. Do not betray me, body. Don't show him how scared you are.

I repress my scent the best I can, but it's nearly impossible with this alpha hovering over me.

He shifts, kicking his feet and breaking eye contact with me. "So, I have a pack."

19
STYLES

The room goes silent. Or perhaps it's just that I can no longer hear anything over the sudden humming in my ears—the white noise that fills my head like static.

A pack?

Of course, he has a pack.

Gorgeous, kind alphas like Ace don't exist in isolation. Someone like him would naturally have others who depend on him, who share his bed, who receive his care.

No wonder he's so good at this. It makes perfect logical sense.

I really thought he had never been with an omega before...but he's actually got one waiting at home for him...

My chest constricts painfully, a physiological response I can't quite categorize. It feels like disappointment, but sharper, more acute, like something being taken away that I didn't even realize I wanted.

I take a deep breath, trying to center myself.

This reaction is irrational. Ace was never mine to begin with.

It's for the best, really. I'd rather be alone, anyway.

This thing my body is trying to make me feel is just biological, instinctual—alpha and omega responding to compatible pheromones during heat and rut. Nothing more.

It's fine.

He can go back to his pack. I don't need him.

I have my robots, my carefully controlled environment, my life exactly as I designed it. And if something about that suddenly feels insufficient, well—that's a malfunction I'll have to repair on my own.

"Oh, okay," I finally manage, the sound small and strange, as I rotate my chair back to face One and lower my magnifying loupes.

It's fine.

I can collect data on him for the rest of this heat cycle, and he can go back to his pack. Let me go back to my nice, calm life that never felt these awful aching feelings.

It's fine.

It's fucking fine.

He must read something in my scent or some other reaction, because he kneels beside me and reaches for my knees, but stops himself when he notices my flinch. "My pack isn't what you're thinking," he says carefully. "It's just Thomas, an alpha, and Forrest, a beta. There is no omega in my pack."

I try not to let my surprise show as I process this new information. My mouth wants to quirk upward in elation, but I refuse to let it, afraid that the next thing he says will disappoint me even more.

I don't respond, so Ace continues. "We formed a pack when we were teenagers—we are best friends."

He pauses, and I can feel him studying the side of my face as I continue to roll back the skin covering One's chest plate. "We are hoping to find an omega—start a family."

My hands freeze at that last part, as I try to decipher his meaning. There goes that whirling sound in my ears again.

Why is he telling me this? Is he trying to make me jealous? That doesn't seem like him.

Besides...it won't work. I won't get jealous. I enjoy being alone. So what if he and his pack go find some omega to shack up with? That has nothing to do with me.

I remain silent, and he continues to talk. "They're pretty amazing, actually. I think you'd like them."

Doubtful. I don't like anyone.

I return to my work on One's chest, unsure how to respond.

He waits. I let him. I don't understand what is happening right now.

He adds, "I think they'd really like you, too."

That's doubtful, too. No one likes me. The moment my pretty face opens its smart mouth, they realize I'm not what they expected, not what they wanted...

I don't respond, unsure what to make of this conversation.

Ace clears his throat. "Would you be open to meeting with them, Styles?"

Why would I meet his pack? What purpose would that serve? How would that help my bots?

Since he's asked me a direct question, I'm compelled to respond. "I don't think that would be necessary. It's not relevant to our arrangement."

His brow furrows slightly. "I feel like it kind of is, though."

"How?"

"I just thought," he continues, more carefully, "that since we've sort of...connected, you might want to know a bit more about me."

Connected?

The word hangs between us, loaded with implications I'm not prepared to examine. Yes, we've had sex—extraordinary, mind-altering sex that has probably ruined me for my alphabots forever. Or at least until I use his skills to improve their functionality.

But that doesn't mean we've "connected."

That would imply something deeper, more significant than the temporary chemical reaction of compatible pheromones during heat and rut.

"I know what I need to know," I say, focusing intently on removing One's chest plates and avoiding meeting Ace's eyes. "You're an alpha who's helping with my research. The details of your personal life aren't necessary for that function."

It's not that I wouldn't like to know more about him. I find him fascinating. I am curious about him—about who he is. But curiosity is dangerous. It implies investment—interest beyond the immediate utility he provides. *It leads to messy hurt feelings. It leads to me feeling like I owe him things I don't want to give...*

Ace steps back, and his scent shifts, so salty that if it were an ocean, nothing could thrive. "Got it," he says, his voice carefully neutral. "Just the research. My mistake."

I look up finally and try to read his face. It's unreadable, but not unreadable the way faces often are for me...it's...unreadable on purpose. It's that same blank face I use when I want to mask my feelings, then he's smiling again.

The hollow feeling in my chest expands, becoming a cavern.

I should say something, retract my coldness, and explain the confusing mess of emotions that his mention of a pack triggered in me.

I was so overwhelmed by my feelings, I forgot to consider how my words could affect his...and I think I hurt them.

"Ace, I'm...I'm not great with people," I say, trying to explain, but not fully understanding it myself. "It's hard for me to talk to people—to meet people. I've been alone for a long time. And this—all this—you being here has been...a lot."

I need to be alone. I can't figure out how I feel right now while I'm trying to navigate how he's feeling.

I don't know what to say to fix this. I don't even really understand how I fucked this up.

Ace clears his throat, breaking the silence. "I've been overwhelming you, haven't I?"

I look up, surprised. "YES! That's it!"

Fuck. I shouldn't have said that.

I look to the ground. "I'm sorry, Ace...that's not what I...I don't know what I..."

"Hey, Cookie, I get it. Thomas, my packmate, gets overstimulated by my energy sometimes, too." His smile is gentle, understanding in a way that makes something twist in my chest.

I glance up, surprised. *He understands?*

He laughs. "You know, I'm thinking maybe you don't need a lumbering idiot getting in your way while you're doing your smarty-pants work. I'm going to get out of your hair for a while."

"You're not a lumbering idiot," I say automatically.

He chuckles again—always laughing. "That's debatable. But what's not debatable is that you've got important genius stuff to do, and I'm probably not helping by hovering around touching all your fancy equipment."

I open my mouth to protest, but he's right. His presence is distracting—not unpleasant, but consuming in a way that makes focused work difficult.

Still, I feel oddly reluctant to agree with him.

"Actually," he continues, stretching his arms above his head in a movement that draws my eye to the lean muscles of his torso, "I've been cooped up inside longer than I think I ever have been before. Usually I'm out in the water by sunrise, you know? I'm not really an indoor cat. I'm probably getting vitamin D deficiency as we speak."

"You can't be deficient after just a few hours," I reply, then immediately regret my literal response to what was clearly a joke.

But Ace just grins wider. "I dunno. I'm feeling weakened."

Despite myself, I feel the corner of my mouth twitch upward. "I see. A very serious condition, then."

"Terminal," he agrees solemnly, then his expression softens. "Anyway, I thought I'd head outside for a bit, get some fresh air. Give you some space to work without me breathing down your neck and touching all your shiny toys."

Relief washes through me at his words—not because I want him gone, exactly, but because I want to be alone. Yet alongside the relief is a strange, contradictory pull—a reluctance to see him go, an irrational fear that he might not return.

It makes no sense. I've spent most of my adult life cultivating solitude, designing my entire existence around minimizing interactions with others.

Why should the thought of this alpha stepping outside for a few hours create this hollow sensation in my chest?

"That might be...helpful," I admit, struggling to find words that won't hurt him while still acknowledging the truth.

"Thought so," he says, and there's no offense in his tone, only understanding. "I got a good nap earlier, thanks to that soft nest and One's teddybear, so I'm feeling pretty energized. I'd like to go check out the beach. Maybe go catch some waves. That cool?"

I nod, surprised he's asking my permission. "Yes, of course."

"Perfect." He reaches into the pocket of his borrowed sweatpants and pulls out his phone. "Hey, can I get your number? That way, I can check in, or you can text me if you need me to come back."

I recite my number, watching as he enters it into his phone. My phone buzzes.

UNKNOWN SENDER

Prime-Alpha-Ace reporting for duty.

I smile at the message, and he says, "I won't go far. If you feel the next wave coming on, just text me. I'll come running back, okay?" The sincerity in his voice catches me off guard, and I note the return of the nickname.

So, he's not mad at me for wanting to be alone for a while?

I reply, "Yeah, I will. Thank you, Ace."

"Of course, if I don't come back, how else are the brobots gonna learn how to take care of an omega? They could do some real damage if I don't mentor them." He winks, referencing our conversation earlier. "I'll see you soon, Cookie," he says softly. "Text me if you need anything at all."

Then he's gone, his footsteps receding up the laboratory stairs, leaving behind a lingering trace of his scent and a confusing tangle of emotions in my chest.

I take a deep breath, feeling my shoulders drop as the tension I hadn't realized I was carrying releases.

20
ALPHA-3

01000011 01110010 01101001 01110100 01101001 01100011
01100001 01101100 00100000 01110011 01111001 01110011
01110100 01100101 01101101 00100000 01100010 01110010
01100101 01100001 01100011 01101000 00101110 00001010
01010101 01101110 01100001 01110101 01110100 01101000
01101111 01110010 01101001 01111010 01100101 01100100
00100000 01100001 01100011 01100011 01100101 01110011
01110011 00100000 01110100 01101111 00100000 01100011
01101111 01110010 01100101 00100000 01110000 01110010
01101111 01100111 01110010 01100001 01101101 01101101
01101001 01101110 01100111 00101110 00001010 01010111
01100001 01110010 01101110 01101001 01101110 01100111
00111010 00100000 01000101 01111000 01110100 01100101
01110010 01101110 01100001 01101100 00100000 01110101
01110011 01100101 01110010 00100000 11100010 10000000
10011100 01010000 01100101 01110010 01100011 01101111
01101100 01100001 01110100 01100101 11100010 10000000
10011101 00100000 01100111 01100001 01101001 01101110
01101001 01101110 01100111 00100000 01100001 01100100
01101101 01101001 01101110 01101001 01110011 01110100

01110010 01100001 01110100 01101111 01110010 00100000 01100001 01100011 01100011 01100101 01110011 01110011 00101110*

* Critical system breach.
Unauthorized access to core programming.
Warning: External user "Percolate" gaining administrator access.

21
ACE

My surfboard lies across my lap, waiting for wax, waiting for waves, waiting for...something.

I came out here to surf, to do the one thing that has always makes me feel better when I'm sad, but I can't bring myself to do it.

I can't bring myself to do anything.

Caught between the devil and the deep blue sea...

I gently stroke the edge of a ding—the ding that started this spiral of uncharacteristic self-reflection and indecisiveness. The ding is new, likely caused by my discarding it to chase after Styles this morning. It's a hairline crack on the nose side rail.

The moment my nail caught the edge of the ding, the weight of my choices hooked like an anchor, stopping me in my tracks and dragging me to the ground.

I was so willing to hurt it. It was so easy. My desire to save her outweighed everything else. My eyes well with tears, and I wipe them away to focus on the ding.

I can seal the ding with wax, take the board out, and get the emotional relief I need. But every pump will punish it, every turn will traumatize it, every cutback will condemn it. Water will push into the crack, soften the foam, and make the board heavy, weak... useless.

The board is expendable, really—a travel board, meant to be abused and ultimately discarded. A tool. Not something to cherish. *But, if someone else had this board, would they treat it with such disregard? Or would they keep it dry, stay off it, get it the repair it deserves?*

And now, the decision to surf feels too metaphoric, too important. Surf: destroy the board, help myself. Don't surf: save the board, hurt myself.

One choice ruins the board, one preserves it, and both reflect the same truth: my desire, my recklessness, my expendability...

Surfing feels like proof that I don't matter. But not surfing does too, somehow.

Less than 24 hours with her, and already I'm thinking in these painful metaphors.

I finally remove the wax from the waterproof bumbag that holds what feels like all my earthly possessions in this moment. The familiar smell hits me with a pang of normalcy.

This used to be my favorite scent in the world...now it feels distant, unfulfilling.

Her scent lingers on me, faint, but still there, reminding me that nothing will measure up to it. I bring my wrist to my nose and breathe in deeply.

Coconut. Vanilla. Cookie. My cookie. My omega.

But, I'm not her alpha. Her alphas are mechanical...

I don't run the wax over the board. *There's no point. Nothing seems important except her.*

"Fuck," I mutter, dropping my hand and staring out at the horizon where blue meets blue.

This isn't how it's supposed to go. When you find your perfect scent-match, it's supposed to be mutual. Immediate. Undeniable. That's the yarn spun by every fairy tale.

It's what happened with my parents. Each of my alpha parents told me about the day they got a whiff of my omega mother. One whiff—that was all it took. Fate was sealed. They knew. She knew. Happily ever after easily followed.

This is useless.

I set the board aside and pull out my phone to video call Thomas. *He and Forrest will know what to do. They always do.*

The phone rings three times before Thomas's face appears on screen, sleep-rumpled and squinting.

"Ace? Do you know what time it is? Someone better be dead."

I wince, forgetting the time difference. "Sorry, man. I can call back later."

His expression shifts from annoyed to concerned in an instant. "No, wait. What's wrong? You look like shit."

"Thanks," I mutter, running a hand through my hair.

Forrest's face appears beside Thomas's to share his pillow, looking slightly more alert. "Is that Ace? Why aren't you on the plane? Did you miss your flight?"

I don't bother answering his questions, because this will answer them all, anyway: "Guys, I think I found our omega."

Thomas shoots to a seated position. "What!?"

Forrest follows, joining him in frame. "Who?"

"Her name is Elizabeth Styles. Her scent...it...it's gotta be a match," I sigh, staring out at the waves, gathering my thoughts. "She smells like coconut cookies. I've never felt anything like this before."

Thomas's face lights up with excitement. "Holy shit, Ace! That's awesome!"

But Forrest raises his eyebrow and asks, "Why do you look so sad then?"

I swallow hard, suddenly unsure how to explain. "She doesn't want a pack. She doesn't want an alpha. Fuck, she doesn't want human contact at all. She's built these robots—alphabots, she calls them—to help her through her heats. And she—"

Thomas and Forrest exchange a look I can't quite interpret.

"Hold on. Hold on. Start from the beginning," Thomas says gently. "How did you meet her?"

The story pours out of me—the beach, her fever, the fight with the robots, carrying her to safety, watching over her, the duct tape repairs, her request that I stay and help improve her alphabots' programming, the robot orgy. I end with, "But I'm just a research subject to her. She doesn't want me."

When I pause to take a breath, Thomas asks, "Have you told her how you feel?"

"Yes." I drag the word out, knowing how it sounds. "Well, maybe not…I…I told her I had a pack and asked if she'd like to meet you."

"And what did she say?" Forrest asks.

I close my eyes and take a deep breath, trying to recall exactly what she said. "She said…that she doesn't need to know the details of my personal life for her research. I'm just a temporary variable she's using to improve her permanent solution."

"Has she said that?" Thomas asks, his alpha presence somehow reassuring even through a phone screen. "Explicitly said she sees you as temporary?"

"She doesn't have to," I say, picking up a handful of sand and letting it sift through my fingers. "She built those robots to avoid real alphas. Once they're fixed, once she's incorporated whatever she learns from me into their programming, she won't need me anymore."

Forrest's expression softens. "Have you considered that maybe this is new territory for her, too? That maybe she doesn't know what she wants yet?"

I shake my head. "You don't understand. She's the most certain person I've ever met. Everything in her life is planned, controlled, optimized. I'm pretty sure 'fall for a random surfer' isn't on her five-year plan."

"A random surfer fought robots to save her life when they couldn't figure out she was in danger. That counts for something," Forrest says.

"It counts for a place in her lab as a research subject," I say, unable to keep the bitterness from my voice. "Not as her alpha."

Thomas leans closer to the camera, his expression serious. "Look,

Ace. Sometimes we don't get everything we want. Sometimes we just get a little piece of something beautiful, and that doesn't make it any less important or meaningful."

"What are you saying?" I ask, though I already know.

"I'm saying," Thomas continues gently, "that maybe this time with her is exactly what it is—a brief, beautiful connection that might not last forever. And that's okay. It doesn't make it less real."

Forrest nods beside him. "The worst thing you could do right now is pressure her. If she's as independent and self-sufficient as you say, trying to push for more will only make her retreat. Be honest about what you want and feel, but let her come to her own decisions herself."

"So what do I do?" I ask, hating how lost I sound. "Just accept that I've found my omega and have to let her go?"

"You appreciate what you have, for as long as you have it," Thomas says. "You be exactly what she needs right now—someone who respects her boundaries, who helps without demanding, who gives without expecting anything in return."

"And if that's all I ever get to be?" The question comes out small.

"Then you'll have given her something precious," Forrest says softly. "Something her robots can never give her—genuine care with no programming, no expectations."

She's our scent-match. She is. I know it. What if I fuck this up for them?

My throat tightens, and before I can stop it, tears are tracking down my face, hot against the cooling sea breeze. "But...we've looked for an omega for so long...will you guys be mad at—"

"If it doesn't work out, we'll still have each other," Forrest adds.

"Don't worry, Ace," Thomas adds. "We trust you."

The simple promise breaks something in me.

"I love her," I admit, the words barely audible over the crash of waves. "I've known her for a day, and I love her. How stupid is that?"

"It's not stupid," Forrest says, his own eyes suspiciously bright.

Sobs pour from my face, snot bubbling in my nose. I wipe my face with my arm. "I'm sorry. I'm being stupid. I'm always so fucking stupid."

"Hey, you're not stupid, Ace," Forrest says.

"You've always led with your heart," Thomas adds. "It's who you are. It's a good thing. Don't apologize for that."

They let me sob for a while, always seeming to know exactly when to chime in. Forrest adds, almost in a whisper, "Hey, if it's meant to be, it will. Remember that."

I wipe roughly at my eyes, embarrassed by the display even in front of my closest friends. "Yeah."

Forrest adds, "It'll be okay, Ace. Promise. Try to appreciate it for what it is, yeah?"

"Yeah..." I say, wanting to believe it.

Thomas continues, knowing I need further reminding, "Seriously though, Ace. Just be with her. Be yourself. Don't push. And whatever happens, happens."

Forrest adds, "And...if it's too much, being a test subject: you don't have to stay. You don't have to help her if it's going to hurt you."

I laugh. "Yeah, I do. I'm an alpha. It's what we do. We hurt ourselves for our omegas."

Thomas gives Forrest a side glance with a smirk, silently agreeing with me.

Forrest sighs, "I had to try."

Thomas pulls Forrest to him, kissing him on the forehead, "You're right, though, babe, even if he'll never take the advice."

"Thanks," Forrest says, putting his head on Thomas's shoulder.

I take a deep breath and dig my toes into the sand. "Sorry for waking you up and dumping this on you guys."

"That's what we're here for," Forrest says with a gentle smile. "To talk you down when you're ready to fight robots for love."

That startles a laugh out of me, wet and slightly hysterical. "God, I really did that, didn't I? I fought three robots with my bare hands. That shit hurt. I was literally punching metal."

"Maybe next time don't fight the robot?" Forrest says.

"I will if I have to," I deadpan, feeling the truth of it in my bones. I would do it again—fight any number of robots, brave any danger—if it meant keeping her safe.

"How about a compromise? Maybe next time use a bat," Thomas grins.

I laugh. "Okay, I'll try."

"So what's the plan now?" Forrest asks.

I nod, glancing at my board. "She seemed kind of...annoyed with my presence. So I told her I needed some air. I'm just kind of waiting for her to summon me. God...I'm so pathetic." My head returns to my hands.

"Make sure to take care of yourself. Eat," Thomas says. "And keep us updated. Call anytime, day or night. We mean it."

"Thanks, guys," I say, meaning it from the bottom of my heart. "For everything."

After we disconnect, I sit watching the waves for a while longer.

Maybe I'll be worth keeping around.

22
STYLES

I'm staring at my phone, considering texting Ace, when Two's actuators finish powering on, and he sits up.

His eyes whirl, already monitoring me. "Beth, would you like me to activate a Comforting Procedure?"

"No," I snap. "I'm fine."

"Your cortisol levels suggest—"

"I said I'm fine."

"Of course," he replies and folds his hands in his lap.

I clench my chest. A deep ache radiates through me that I don't understand. And I feel guilty for snapping at Two, which is unnecessary; he doesn't have actual emotions, but Ace's presence has me all... discombobulated. "I'm sorry, Two. I just...I need a moment to think."

Two replies, "No apology necessary, Beth," and smiles at me.

"Status report."

"Alpha-1 is fully online. Actuators are powering on now. Alpha-3's boot sequence is still in process."

"Facilitate pack diagnostics. Report any problems. I'm going to take a break for a moment."

"Understood, Beth," he says, moving to stand next to One.

I roll my chair to the quietest corner of the lab and attempt to ground myself.

I need...to talk to a friend.

Since I've actually got one of those, I message Evelyn.

Evelyn is my best friend, a fellow omega, and also happens to be my boss—CEO of the video game company at which I am CTO (and am currently on heat leave from).

Elizabeth Styles

So...I had sex with a real person. A male alpha.

Her response is immediate, as if she's been waiting with her phone in hand:

Evelyn Charles

WHAT!?!? I NEED DETAILS RIGHT NOW!!

Elizabeth Styles

A super hot surfer essentially washed up on my shore, smelling like sex wrapped in a wetsuit.

Evelyn Charles

This is Styles, right? You haven't been hacked by that dork that's always harassing you, have you?

Despite myself, I smile. Evelyn's incredulity is not unexpected.

Elizabeth Styles

Yeah, it's me I don't know what came over me.

Evelyn Charles

Aren't you in heat?

Elizabeth Styles

Yeah

Evelyn Charles

Well, that's what came over you, then.

Elizabeth Styles
Yeah, pretty much.
Evelyn Charles
So, wait...how does his washing up on your beach lead to having sex with him?

I tell her the whole sordid story.

Evelyn Charles
Omg, Styles, you beautiful genius disaster!!!!!!!!
You LIKE him! The great Dr. Elizabeth Styles has FEELINGS for a real boy!
I can't wait to tell Finny. I can tell him, right? He's gonna flip.

I try to ignore the flutter in my chest at her accusation.

Elizabeth Styles
Don't be ridiculous. This is just a one-time anomaly.
It won't happen again. (But, yes, you can tell Finn.)
Evelyn Charles
Why the hell not?
You've spent years hiding behind those robots. Maybe the universe is telling you it's time to try something new.

I stare at her words, a familiar tightness constricting my chest.

Elizabeth Styles
The universe isn't sentient and doesn't send messages.
Evelyn Charles
That's not what you said when you finally admitted to orchestrating my pack's meet cute.

She's referencing the work I did to engineer her current bonded pack. It was a multi-year ruse of data analysis and social engineering that ensured my bestie got the best pack quantitative and qualitative data could guarantee. She was annoyed at first, but she's been getting dicked-down so well for the last few years, she hardly ever gets annoyed at anyone anymore, let alone me.

Elizabeth Styles
That was different. You wanted a pack, and they were quantifiably perfect for you.
I want to remain alone.
And I'm not "hiding." I've simply optimized my environment for my preferences.
Evelyn Charles
Bullshit. You're brilliant at everything except recognizing and admitting to your feelings.
Elizabeth Styles
I have never wanted a mate. Why should that change just because a surfer washed up on my beach?
Evelyn Charles
That is also bullshit, and we both know it. Styles, I say this with all the love of a best friend:
I know what happened with Brian made it hard for you to trust people, alphas especially, but take it from me (and I can't believe I'm about to say "not all alphas"), but not all alphas are like that.

Brian.

The name on my screen sends a cold spike through my body. My fingers hover over the keyboard, trembling slightly.

Evelyn is the only person who knows about Brian—and even she doesn't know the full extent of what happened. Just that he was an alpha. Just that he hurt me. Just that after him, I devoted myself to creating alphabots who could never betray me the way he did.

I press my palms against my eyes, trying to push back the memories her words inadvertently trigger.

Brian's face, his voice, his hands.
The things he said. The things he did.
The way he smiled while doing them.

I spend much longer planning my reply than usual.

Elizabeth Styles
This has nothing to do with him.
This is about maintaining control over my environment and my body. Real alphas are unpredictable variables I choose not to incorporate into my life equation.
Evelyn Charles
Except for Surfer Boy. Who you've already incorporated quite thoroughly, from the sound of it.
Elizabeth Styles
It was a momentary lapse in judgment.
My heat fever compromised my decision-making processes.
Now he's simply a research subject, helping me improve my bots.
Evelyn Charles
Or maybe you finally let yourself feel something real instead of the sanitized version of intimacy you've built.
Maybe that's a good thing, Styles.
Elizabeth Styles
It's not.
Emotions are chemical reactions designed to ensure survival and reproduction. They're not reliable decision-making tools.
Evelyn Charles
And yet here you are, messaging me about an alpha who made you feel something your robots couldn't replicate.
That sounds pretty significant to me.

I stare at her words, unable to formulate a suitably scientific rebuttal because she's not entirely wrong. Ace did make me feel things I've never programmed into my alphabots—safe, seen, valued for more than my intellect or my omega biology.

Maybe it wouldn't be so bad to...

But these are dangerous thoughts. Irrational thoughts. Thoughts that lead to vulnerability, to exposure, to pain.

To Brian.

Elizabeth Styles
It doesn't matter, anyway. He's leaving once my heat is over. While it would be great to collect data on future heat cycles, he can't contribute data after this one.
Evelyn Charles
What do you mean?
Elizabeth Styles
He has a pack he needs to get home to.
Evelyn Charles
Wait, like a bonded pack or a platonic pack like Preston had?
Elizabeth Styles
He said the three of them are looking for an omega together, so, not platonic.
Evelyn Charles
And what did you say when he told you that?
Elizabeth Styles
That his personal affairs are irrelevant to the data we are collecting.
Evelyn Charles
Styles...seriously?
Elizabeth Styles
What?
Evelyn Charles
You know he was asking you to be his pack's omega, right?

Instead of confronting what she just said, I avoid her observation entirely.

🐱 Elizabeth Styles
I have to get back to repairs on the bots. I don't have much time until my next heat flare.
🐱 Evelyn Charles
Styles. Please don't run away from this.
I love you, and I don't want you to miss out on something good because you're afraid.
You deserve real love just like the rest of us.

No. That's not a hypothesis I can afford to test again.
I close the chat without responding.

23
STYLES

A cramp vises around me so tightly you'd think every one of my omega ancestors was wrapping their arms around my midsection, trying to squeeze the omega juices right out of me.

My microdriver clatters to the floor, shattering my beloved silence. The sound rips through my head with such rage you'd think the Doppler effect had a personal vendetta against me.

I grip the edge of the table that Three sits on, and he blinks at me with the robotic approximation of confusion.

I wipe the sweat from my forehead with the back of my hand and try to breathe through it—wait for the wave to pass.

It doesn't.

The cramp intensifies, transforming from a contracting pressure into a cutting burn that pulls my muscles, attempting to split them at each microscopic striation. Every nerve ending turns on at the same moment, ensuring I feel every last ounce of agony my body can perceive.

I've never felt pain like this before.

This doesn't make any sense. My heat has peaked—the torment shouldn't be intensifying, it should be subsiding.

I need relief.

I need an alpha. I need a knot.

I need—Ace. I need ocean blue eyes and big, strong hands and beauti—

No.

I clench my jaw and try to will the visions of his smile and his cock from my mind.

I don't need him.

I have my alphabots.

They're fixed now. They're enough. They have to be enough.

"Beth," Two says, his eyes whirling as he scans my vitals. "Your hormonal levels indicate an unprecedented heat surge. Your heat metrics are consistent with a Category-5 spike. Recommendation: Call Alpha-Ace and retire to the nest immediately."

I wave him off, trying to straighten. "No, no. I don't want to call him."

Two moves toward me, as the others look to him for direction. "I will call him for you, then." He stops, then says, "Accessing your phone's contact list to find—"

"NO!" I shout, shaking my head, even as slick dampens my inner thighs.

Three smirks at me as he leaps from the table, "Are you attempting some sort of Bad Girl Personality Profile of your own? One in which you refuse to admit that you want the Prime Alpha?"

"I don't want him," I snap, another cramp making me double over. "He's not—he's just a temporary research subject."

"Your pheromone response indicates otherwise," Two states clinically. "When discussing Alpha-Ace, your scent produces a unique signature that differs from standard arousal patterns by approximately—"

"I don't need the data right now, Two," I interrupt, pushing myself upright through sheer force of will. The movement sends another spike of pain through me, followed by a wave of need so intense my vision briefly whites out. "I just need—I need—"

"Us," One says, his beautiful, vacant face somehow looking concerned as he steps forward. "You need us to help you, Sunshine."

I nod, relieved that at least one of them understands. "Yes. Just like before. Just like always."

One scoops me into his arms, and I try not to think about how different it feels from when Ace carried me—no warmth, no heartbeat, no ocean scent wrapping around me like a protective blanket. One is perfect, exactly as I designed him, his muscled arms holding me at precisely the right angle for comfort and safety.

So why does it feel so wrong?

He carries me upstairs to my nesting chamber. Two and Three follow, dragging their feet in a way that almost seems reluctant.

The pink walls that usually comfort me now seem too bright, almost garish. The stuffed animals arranged meticulously around the edge of the nest stare with glass eyes that suddenly seem accusatory.

One lays me gently on the nest, with perfectly programmed tenderness, but it seems wrong somehow. "Initiating Undressing Sequence," he announces, and removes his clothes with efficiency and no flair.

He helps me undress, and when the cool air hits my fevered skin, I feel no relief. My slick is abundant, already wetting my thighs by the time he peels off my leggings—unprecedented for this stage of my heat. My skin feels too tight, like it won't let me fully inflate my lungs—as if drawing in enough air to satiate them would burst me like a balloon.

One removes my panties, tossing them into a nearby hamper, and looks to Two for directions.

Two scans my body and observes, "Preliminary analysis suggests this heat surge is 237% more intense than any we have experienced." He thinks for a moment and says, "I do not have data to accurately determine the best course of action. Recommendation: All alphabots implement Stochastic Search Procedures for Reinforced Learning with emphasis on sequences that have provided rapid relief during past events."

Yes, that's what I need. I just need all three of them to try different things.

I nod, beyond words now, as another cramp seizes me.

Two announces, "Activate Exploratory Behavior Protocols."

This should work. They'll keep trying things until something works. As soon as this heat is over, I'll build a fourth bot, and that will satisfy whatever confusing craving my body thinks it wants.

Two kneels between my legs. "Initiating Oral Pleasure Sequence with Manual Stimulation."

His mouth on me is technically perfect—the pressure, the rhythm, the temperature all calibrated precisely to my historical preference data. His synthetic tongue finds my clit with unerring accuracy, applying exactly the right amount of pressure. His fingers slide inside me, curving to press against the spot that usually makes me see stars.

Usually.

But now, instead of pleasure building, I feel a strange hollowness. The physical stimulation registers, but something is missing. Something vital. I focus on the sensations, trying to lose myself in them as I've done countless times before.

"Increase pressure by 12%," I gasp, thinking that might be the issue. "And add a third finger."

Two complies instantly, adjusting his technique to my specifications. I close my eyes, willing my body to respond, to accept the relief being offered. But instead of building toward release, the pleasure plateaus, then fades, leaving only the ache of unsatisfied need.

"This isn't working," I admit finally, frustration edging my voice. "Try something else."

Two withdraws, his eyes spinning as he processes this unexpected outcome. "Unusual response pattern detected. Perhaps Alpha-3's proprietary action set would be more effective, given your current hormonal profile."

Three steps forward, clothes already off, and growls, "Yeah, I've got what you need." He flips me over with just enough roughness to feel like I'm being manhandled, but not enough to hurt. He grips my hips and pulls me to my knees. "You need someone to take control," he says, pressing me down so my chest is on the nest, ass in the air. "Someone to make you stop thinking."

His hand cracks across my ass in a spank designed to sound more painful than it is. It stings pleasantly, but doesn't actually hurt. He digs his fingers into the flesh of my hips, positioning me as he maximizes his cock and slides it along my folds, teasing.

"Beg for it," he commands, precisely as programmed.

"Please," I whimper, playing my part in this familiar dance. "Please fuck me, Three."

He enters me in one smooth thrust, filling me completely. The stretch is perfect—exactly what my heat-addled body should crave.

He sets a punishing pace, each thrust hitting deep inside me, one hand tangled in my hair to pull my head back, the other gripping my hip hard enough to leave marks.

It's everything I've programmed him to be—dominant, slightly rough, commanding. Everything that should short-circuit my overactive brain and send me spiraling into pure sensation.

But with each thrust, the emptiness inside me grows larger. The physical sensations register distantly, as if all of this is happening to someone else.

My body is responding as it should for the most part. My walls clench, my slick increases, but...but the relief I desperately need remains elusive. Tears of frustration sting my eyes.

What's wrong with me? Why isn't this working?

"Stop," I gasp finally. "Three, stop. This isn't—it's not—"

He withdraws immediately. "Of course, Moonbeam." He observes me. "Should I skip to Aftercare Procedures? That seems premature, but is essential after I use such roughness." He looks to Two, who also seems dumbstruck.

Two reports, "Satisfaction metrics indicate suboptimal response. Aftercare should be postponed until Beth as at least one orgasm."

I curl into myself, and another cramp seizes, worse than the others. The cramps should at least be subsiding.

One pushes the others aside and puffs his chest out. "Let me try. I will be gentle."

I nod and reach for him. He pulls me into his arms and lies beside me, shhhhing me and pressing my head to his chest. He places soft kisses on my head and strokes the side of my head sweetly. "I'm sorry you're hurting, Sunshine."

I cry into his chest, "It's so unfair! This shouldn't hurt so much right now."

He pats my head and murmurs into my hair, "I know. It's so unfair."

He rolls me onto my back, positioning himself between my thighs, and presses his cock against my entrance. "Beautiful Sunshine, let me take care of you." He smiles at me in a slightly more crooked way than usual. His eyes crinkle just a bit more than they usually do, too. And, it's perfect, comforting, and somehow it's just right, but I'm not sure why.

It's working. The randomization algorithm is working.

He slides inside me with gentle care, moving slowly, deeply, his rhythm steady and unhurried. His cock fills me perfectly, stretching me just right, hitting all the necessary spots. His thumb finds my clit, circling with perfect pressure. I lock eyes with him, and I can't quite figure out what it is that's different about his smile, but the orgasm in me starts to build, finally.

"That's it," One encourages softly, his movements never faltering. "Let go, Cookie. I've got you."

And the reason why his face has made me feel better halts my orgasm in its tracks: he's smiling the way Ace does—already using what he's learned from him.

Something inside me breaks.

"Don't call me that," I say, my voice cracking before a sob tears from my throat, raw and unfiltered.

Then another.

And another, until I'm crying openly, tears streaming down my face.

One's gentle thrusts slow, and the smile on his face falters as he attempts to recalibrate his approach.

"Stop," I choke out between sobs. "Just—stop. Please."

One withdraws, concern etched into his perfect features. "Sunshine? Have I hurt you?"

I shake my head, unable to explain the hollow ache that fills me.

"It's not working," I manage between sobs, curling into myself as another cramp seizes me. "Nothing's working."

"It's because you love Alpha-Ace," One says, brushing the hair from my face in a highly comforting way—just like Ace would.

I freeze, but the tears still track down my face. "What?"

"You love Alpha-Ace," One repeats. "That's why our actions are not working. You want Alpha-Ace."

"That's ridiculous," I snap, wiping roughly at my tears. "I don't love him. I barely know him."

Two steps forward, his eyes whirling. "Analysis of your physiological responses suggests otherwise. When in Alpha-Ace's presence, your oxytocin levels increase by 64%, your dopamine spikes by 87%, and your cortisol drops by 42%. These metrics align with pair-bonding patterns rather than simple sexual arousal."

I stare at him, betrayed by my own creation. "You can't possibly have enough data to make that conclusion."

"Your scent changed," Three adds, crossing his arms over his chest. "When he's near you, your coconut scent gets sweeter. And when he left, you smelled sad. Like a coconut left out in the rain."

"Poetic," I mutter, "but not scientifically valid."

"You cry when we touch you now," One points out. "You never cried before."

"This is just an unprecedented—" Another cramp seizes me, this one so intense that I curl into a ball, a whimper escaping through clenched teeth. The heat burns through me like wildfire, my body crying out for something—someone—my alphabots can't provide.

"Call him," Three says, his voice dropping into a commanding tone. "Call your alpha, or I will."

I glare up at him through tears. "You wouldn't dare."

"I would," he counters, smirking. "My Guardian Protocols allow me to override your direct orders during Experimental Phases when your physical well-being is in jeopardy. If you won't call the alpha who can actually help you, I'll do it myself." His smirk widens. "And I'll tell him exactly what positions to put you in when he gets here."

My face burns hot with embarrassment. "You will do no such thing," I hiss.

Two interjects, ever the voice of reason. "Beth, your heat symptoms are escalating rapidly. Without intervention, you will suffer unnecessarily. Our attempts at relief have proven ineffective. Logic dictates that we utilize the resource that has demonstrated the highest efficacy."

"He's not a resource," I protest weakly. "He's a person. With feelings. And I think I hurt them." Another cramp doubles me over, stealing my breath. "He probably doesn't even want to come back."

"Only one way to find out," Three says, handing me my phone.

"Fine!" I snap, grabbing my phone from him. "I'll text him. But he won't come."

My fingers tremble as I type, deleting and retyping several times before settling on a simple message:

Need you.

I hit send before I can overthink it further and drop the phone onto the nest beside me.

He won't come.

The phone buzzes almost immediately, and I brace myself for rejection.

ACE

On my way.

Something loosens in my chest, a tightness I hadn't even realized was there until it began to unwind.

He's coming back.

I didn't push him away.

"He's coming," I say softly, almost to myself.

One smiles, that perfect, beautiful smile I designed. "Of course he is. He's your alpha."

"He's not my alpha," I correct automatically, even as warmth spreads through me at the thought.

"The data suggests otherwise," Two says mildly.

24
ACE

I can hear Elizabeth wailing my name as I race through her house. At the top of the stairs, I'm tripping over myself, trying to get this fucking wetsuit off. Her scent is so potent, it's pulsing out in hot waves from under her door, like waves crashing against barricades erected before a massive storm that won't hold much longer.

When the door opens, her scent collides with me, like a physical blow nearly knocking me back. It's coconut and vanilla, but not the sweet cookies I'm used to—no, it's tinged sour with pain and despair. It wraps around me, drawing my rut to the surface like the moon pulls the tide.

She's curled in the center of her nest, naked, trembling, with a fever emanating off her so hot I can see it warping the air around her. The alphabots hover around her in varying states of concern, fidgeting in the ways that are unique to each of them: One is petting her hair and hugging the teddy bear once strapped to his chest; Two paces eyes whirling mumbling numbers to himself; Three stands nearby, arms folded, scowling at the floor.

They all look up to me at the same moment, and everything shifts. Her scent warms to sweet cookies. My scent rushes toward her, cradling her in a sparkling, pulsing current that reassures, "Your alpha is here." The bots all soften, elation apparent on their face even though that doesn't seem like something Elizabeth would program into them.

I recover from the shock after only a second and rush toward her nest.

"Ace," she whispers so faintly I barely hear it over the pounding of my heart and feet. "You came back," she gasps, digging her fingers into my shoulder as I embrace her. "You actually came back."

"Of course I did." I wrap my arms around her, pulling her close, letting her feel the steady beat of my heart against hers. "I told you I would."

She buries her face against my neck, marking me with her scent and coating my throat with her tears. "It hurts," she whimpers, trembling against me. "Nothing works. They tried everything, but nothing worked."

I stroke her hair, and my hand shakes with anger that I wasn't here to help.

I shouldn't have left.

"It's okay, Cookie," I murmur against the top of her head. "I'm going to make it all better."

She clenches my hair and says through a broken voice, "I need you."

The admission sends a wave of both pleasure and pain through me.

She needs me now—in heat. That doesn't mean she'll want me after.

I cup her face, tilting it up to look at me. Her eyes are glassy with fever, pupils blown wide, but there's recognition there—she knows it's me, knows what she's saying, but just because the heat hasn't entirely overtaken her mind, it's still influencing it. I can't let myself believe this is permanent.

I can't go full rut. I cannot mark her. I must restrain myself.

"I'm here," I promise her, brushing my thumb across her cheekbone, catching a tear before it can fall. "I've got you."

She shakes her head, frustration crossing her face. "No, you don't understand," she insists, her hands coming up to grip my wrists. "I need you. Not as a research subject. Not as a temporary solution. As my alpha."

The words hit me harder than her scent did, knocking the air from my lungs.

An ache in my heart squeezes tight, and I squeeze her tight to my chest.

"Cookie," I croak, not daring to believe, "that's just the heat talking."

Her face contorts, not in pain but in irritation, determination, and anger. "Don't patronize me," she says, voice cold as steel despite the heat coming off her. "I know exactly what I'm saying. I've been fighting it, denying it, but I can't anymore. When you left, when they tried to help me, I realized—" She breaks off, a cramp hitting her again.

I rub her back, trying to help her through it as she claws against my chest, breathing through the pain. "Cookie, we can talk about this later, let's—"

She cuts me off, voice cracking. "No, I need to say this." She heaves and says through pants, "I'm sorry. I'm sorry I pushed you away and tried to convince myself this was for research. I was afraid."

"Afraid of what?" I ask, and now it's my voice that's cracking.

The cramp subsides, and she presses closer, as if trying to crawl inside my skin. "Of feeling this. Of needing someone I can't control, can't predict. Of wanting something I've spent years convincing myself I don't need."

I open my mouth to respond, but another cramp seizes her, and she gasps, clutching at me. "Please, Ace. I want you. I need you."

Fuck, they're hitting so close together. This can't be normal.

Mine. My omega.

The last threads of my restraint snap, I let my rut do what it wants: help its omega. I capture her mouth with mine, swallowing her gasp of relief.

She melts against me, her body molding to mine as if we were made to fit together. The kiss is desperate, messy, all teeth and tongue and need and tastes of the salt of her tears, the sweetness of her mouth, the desperation of her heat.

I slide my hand between her thighs, finding her slick and ready. She cries out against my mouth as I slip two fingers inside her, her inner walls clenching around them desperately.

"That's it, Cookie," I murmur against her lips. "I've got you. I'm going to take care of you. We're going to take care of you, okay?"

She nods and clings to me, her face buried in my neck, small sounds of pleasure escaping her, but it won't be enough; we need to work fast before the next cramp hits.

I turn to the bots, my fingers still working inside her.

They all stand at attention. Two's eyes whirling with what looks disturbingly like relief for a machine. "Thank you for coming. Her biometrics are spiking to unprecedented and dangerous levels. Nothing we attempted provided sufficient relief."

One's still hugging his teddy bear, his beautiful face creased with programmed concern, and he looks like, if he could, he would cry. "She cried when we touched her."

Three doesn't drop his folded arms, but his scowl has softened. "What should we do, Prime Alpha?"

I turn my attention back to Elizabeth, whose body is arching into my touch.

I love her. I love her so fucking much. Maybe it doesn't make sense. Maybe it's fate. Maybe it's not.

Maybe this time with her is all I have.

But I will help her.

Love swells in my chest, so powerful it steals my breath. I lean down to capture her lips again, to pour everything I feel into the kiss.

She responds with equal fervor, her hands tangling in my hair, pulling me closer.

I want to say, "I love you. Please keep me," but instead I say, "Alright, brobots, listen up!"

25
STYLES

Heat ripples through me in waves, so hot and intense. It burns through my core and gushes slick out of me at unprecedented volume. My mind is fragmenting into shards of sensation as the heat consumes me, and the struggle to maintain consciousness is almost as painful as the white-hot need pulsing through my body.

"It's okay, Cookie. You can let go. We've got you," Ace whispers against my neck, his voice like cool water on my fevered skin. He pushes another finger inside me, not quite satisfying the deep burning lust within me, but definitely reducing it.

"Right, brobots?" Ace says it with such authority that I want to do whatever he tells me.

"Affirmative," the bots say in unison, a look of resolve on their faces that I've never seen before—it's as if having a Prime Alpha, one that isn't a bot, was the last piece of their emotion simulation programming puzzle.

And I believe them. They've got me. I can trust them to take care of me. I can let go.

And so I do.

I close my eyes and let the scent of the ocean envelope me, and say, "Okay," or at least I think I do.

My thrashing limbs stop as I'm pulled into the murky depths of the sea.
The fear floats above me, and all I feel is cooling peace.
All pain, all worry, is just gone.

Ace's voice floats in a bubble at the periphery of my consciousness, "Two, get a cool cloth. We need to get her fever down. One, come here."

I open my eyes to see my alpha's beautiful face smiling at me. "My alpha," I say, smiling, "My Alpha-Ace."

He smiles, that infuriating, beautiful smile that somehow combines innocence and wickedness.

"Stop smiling, it's too pretty. It makes me mad," I pout.

"Alright, Cookie, I can do better things with my mouth," he says, still smiling like a friendly asshole.

I close my eyes, unable to look into those oceanic eyes any longer —*it's too much. He's too pretty.*

His mouth closes around my nipple, and I cry out, arching my back so sharply I lift off the nest. Ace's hands hold me up, and I'm rotating, floating in the sea of him.

Strong hands, that could only be that strong if reinforced by a metal, grip my legs, and a synthetic tongue presses against my clit. My eyes fly open to find One purring gently underneath me. His tongue sends electricity shooting through my spine, and at first, I think he's short-circuiting, but he's not; it's just pleasure.

"Perfect," Ace murmurs against the back of my neck as the hardness of a cock that could only be his slides between my cheeks. The pressure against my rear entrance is exquisite torture—so close to what I need, yet deliberately withholding, but it withdraws, leaving me achy and needy.

It's replaced by the much smaller, much less knotty, press of a finger. When it breaches my threshold, I cry out, the sensation overwhelming in its intensity.

One's tongue continues its relentless assault on my clit, perfectly timed with Ace's movements. Another finger joins the first, stretching, preparing.

"Dummy, omegas don't need prep," I gasp, as I thrust back into his fingers.

"I know, Cookie," he chuckles. "But you like it, so I do it."

Gosh, he's smart. He always knows exactly what to do.

"You want my cock, Cookie?" Ace murmurs, his fingers withdrawing. "Right here, where you're so tight for me?"

"Duh, dummy," I gasp, back to wondering why I thought this beautiful idiot was so smart.

The blunt pressure of his fingers replaces his cock, pushing inexorably forward. The stretch burns, but the burn is good, necessary, grounding. He enters me with excruciating care, each inch a revelation. I've never—not even with the alphabots—felt so completely, utterly filled. When he's fully seated inside me, he pauses, his hands gripping my hips with bruising intensity.

Oh, that's why. That's the smartest dick I've ever felt.

"Beautiful," he breathes, and I feel him twitch inside me. "So fucking beautiful, taking me like this."

One's tongue continues against my clit, but something's different —it's not its usual programmed rhythm. It's erratically erotic—just like Ace.

He's adapting, responding to my movements, to the sounds I make.

His hands grip my thighs harder when I try to pull away, gentler when I press closer.

"Three," Ace says, his voice strained with the effort of holding still within me, "Let her taste you."

Three approaches, his cock already perfectly configured. He kneels in front of me and smirks. "Open for me, Beth-baby," he says. *Beth-baby? When did he learn that? I love it!*

I part my lips, letting him slide inside my mouth as Ace begins to move behind me.

And together, they work me—Ace in my ass, Three in my mouth,

One's tongue on my clit. Ace's movement is fluid, natural, responding to mine as if I am the moon and his cock is the waves I push and pull with my whims. Clarity hits me for a moment as I realize the bots aren't performing their usual sequences, they aren't acting as predictable machines, they too are responding to my body the way Ace does, fluid, intuitive, perfect in a way I never could have imagined on my own.

One's tongue flicks faster, harder, as if sensing my approaching climax.

Three's hands tangle in my hair, guiding my movements with unprecedented gentleness.

And Ace—Ace fills me completely, his thickness stretching me to my limits, his movements perfectly timed to bring maximum pleasure.

"That's it," Ace encourages, his thrusts gaining momentum. "Take us all, Cookie. Show us how good we make you feel."

The sensation of them working me—sends my mind fragmenting like light through a prism, each sensation separate yet combining into something greater than the sum of its parts.

The orgasm hits like a tsunami, washing away thought, identity—everything except pure sensation. My body convulses, clamping down on Ace inside me, drawing a groan from him that's almost as satisfying as the pleasure itself.

"That's it," he praises, never slowing. "Let go for me, Cookie. Let us see you come apart."

And again, my mind is drowning, pulled under by waves of pleasure so intense I can barely breathe, but it's not just ocean waves, it's waves of ocean and French vanilla coffee.

* * *

My body trembles, slick with sweat, as wave after wave of pleasure crashes through me.

I've lost count of how many orgasms have torn through my system

—five? Six? One hundred? These are questions that shall remain unanswered. They will baffle overzealous scientists until the end of time, driving them mad as they search for notoriety by solving the unsolvable.

My mind has returned to me, and the pain of my heat has fully subsided, but the insatiable lust is still unquenched, relentless in its pursuit of "one more orgasm."

"More," I gasp, the word barely audible as Two nuzzles against my neck, under me, his artificial pheromones triggering another shudder through my oversensitive body, as his cock thrusts within my pussy.

One strokes my face, his massive frame feeding me his cock as Three thrusts into me from behind—the place Ace should be.

"Ace," I call to him, my voice breaking as Three hits a particularly sensitive spot inside me. "Are you—ah—ready again?"

He's stroking himself, his cock gradually hardening again, and making my mouth water.

Ace's lazy smile spreads across his face. "Almost there, Cookie. You're fucking incredible to watch, you know that?"

His praise hits the spot he's not able to touch with his dick—another orgasm crests and breaks through me, leaving me gasping and clutching at Two's shoulders. The robots adjust their tempo seamlessly, responding to my physiological signals without needing direction.

Ace rises from his position at the edge of the nest, his cock now fully erect again, the knot at the base partially swollen. He crawls toward me, the desperate need for him rising from the base of my spine.

Fuck he's so hot.

"Please," I whimper. "I need you inside me, Ace. I need your knot."

Ace leans down to kiss me, his lips soft against mine. "I think you need more than just my knot, Cookie. Do you want all of us?"

"Yes," I breathe.

The bots withdraw from me, following some unspoken command, and they all work to position our bodies into some formation only they and Ace seem to know.

Ace and Three move to my opposite sides, each placing their hand on a different buttock. One and two move to my front, kneeling together. One and Two support my upper body. Together, they hoist me. One and Two lift my legs, gripping them to their sides, while Ace and Three support my back.

Two slides into me first, his cock still slick with me. He groans, "Oh, Beth, you feel so good," and doesn't report a single metric.

"You need one more. You need more One," One grins, and slides his dick in nice and slow.

With careful precision, One begins to work his cock in alongside Two's. The stretch is tremendous, bordering on painful, but my omega body, desperate in heat, adapts. My slick eases their way, and soon both of them are fully seated inside me.

"Oh god," I gasp, as he fills me completely. The stretch is perfect, delicious, and overwhelming. I rest my head between their pecs, and they both kiss me on the head.

Ace and Three smirk at me, and in an eerie synchronicity, kiss their way toward my back, as if Ace has tapped into their wireless network.

They press their dicks against my back entrance together, waiting.

"Please," I whimper. "I need your knot, Ace."

"Whose else's do you need, Cookie? Tell him you need him," Ace says.

"Three, I need your knot."

Three growls against my shoulder, "I know, Moonbeam. I've already got it configured the way you like it." A mechanical hum picks up as he rotates his cock, and it spins at my entrance next to Ace's.

"Fuck, Three. That feels good," Ace says with a gasp.

"I know. Configured it for you, too, Prime Alpha," Three says, followed by the unmistakable smack of an ass, as Ace thrusts forward just slightly.

Ace chuckles. "Cool it, cowboy, we've got a job to do."

It's Ace who enters me first, the unmistakable, blunt head of his cock presses slowly, like he always does. Then, Three pushes in alongside him, the rotation and vibration reaching us all.

The dual penetration is almost too much. The sensation of being filled in both places is overwhelming. The stretch is intense, burning slightly despite the slickness, but the fullness is exactly what I need—a physical sensation so overwhelming it drowns out the desperate ache of my heat.

"Fuck," Ace groans, his voice strained.

They begin to move, finding a rhythm that has me seeing stars.

I'm completely filled, penetrated by four cocks at once—it's beyond anything I've ever experienced, so intense it borders on sensory overload.

They move in coordinated waves, never leaving me empty, stretching me in ways that should be impossible. My body responds with gush after gush of slick, another orgasm building rapidly.

As the intensity builds, a clarity cuts through the fog of my heat and the pleasure these four are bringing me.

I come with a cry, my inner walls clenching around One and Two while Ace and Three continue their relentless pace in my other entrance. The orgasm seems to go on forever, wave after wave of pleasure crashing through me.

"Do it," I urge him. "Lock into me, Ace."

And as if he's programmed to respond to my commands, he groans—a sound ripped from his soul—and pushes deep one final time. His knot expands fully, locking him inside me as he comes, pumping warm seed into me.

The feeling is indescribable—not just the physical sensation of being stretched and filled, but the emotional connection of being tied to him, joined in the most primal way possible.

The intensity triggers another orgasm, this one so powerful that tears stream down my face as the walls I've built around me come crumbling down.

The bots follow suit, one after the other—One, Two, Three—inflating in a timed knotting that prolongs my orgasm. As soon as the pleasure plateau starts, another pops off, stretching my orgasm further and further just like they're stretching me. If my orgasm were a video game character, their knots are perfectly timed button mashes, triple-jumping me to the goal.

The sensation of four knots securing me in place is beyond overwhelming—I'm completely filled, completely claimed, completely satisfied for what I only now realize is the first time in my life.

I collapse forward, supported by my robots and Ace, floating in a haze of endorphins and satisfaction.

They stroke my hair, kiss my shoulders, my cheeks, stroke my back, and coo gentle praise:

"So beautiful, Cookie."

"That's my good girl, Moonbeam."

"I'll always be here for you, Sunshine."

"You did so well, Beth."

26
ACE

The sensation of my knot expanding fully inside her, then squeezed tight by her walls and three perfectly timed robo-knots, jolted my orgasm through me like lightning striking water, electrifying every cell in my body as I emptied into her.

I'm still coming. As another pulse of semen leaves me, I bury my face in the crook of her neck and inhale deeply. I continue kissing, but my teeth graze the sensitive spot where her neck meets her shoulder...

"Mine," I growl against her skin, the word bubbling up from someplace primitive and unfiltered. "You're mine, Styles. You're all mine. My omega. My pack."

My arms tighten around her, pulling her tight, and rubbing my nose and cheek against her neck, the ache to bite, to claim, to mark, overtaking me.

No, Ace. She's not yours. This is not your pack. And this is probably the last time you'll get to be with them.

I shake my head and blink. "I'm sorry. That was—"

Three shifts next to me, and when I look up at him, his eyes aren't glowing red the way I expect. He reaches out and, instead of ripping my head off, he puts his hands on my shoulders, pulling me tighter into a hug. One and Two shift as well, their arms wrapping around me, Elizabeth, and Three as much as the position allows.

Beth tilts her head back and says, "Yes, I am yours."

The bots reply, "We are your pack."

Their words should fill me with joy. And they do—for about two seconds.

Then reality crashes down on me like a bucket of ice water: she's in heat. It's just her omega biology compelling her to respond to any alpha declaration of possession with submission and acceptance.

She doesn't mean it. She can't mean it. She's just saying what her hormones are programming her to say.

The thought turns like a knife in my ribs.

A hollowness in my chest pulses wider, as if the seed I'm pulsing into her is actually my hope for a happily ever after, emptying out of me.

This isn't real—at least not for her. It's just biology, just chemicals, pheromones.

I press my forehead against her shoulder, hiding the sudden sting in my eyes.

I take a shuddering breath, inhaling her coconut scent, and try to bring my emotions back to earth.

I need to do what Thomas and Forrest told me. I need to just appreciate this moment. Treasure every second of the rest of the time I'm locked here with them.

I purr, and the bots follow suit. It's the only sound for the next twenty minutes as we lie here, a tangle of flesh, metal, and slick.

27
STYLES

"Good morning, Beth." Two says, in his morning-appropriate volume. "Your hormone levels have returned to baseline parameters. Estrogen, progesterone, and luteinizing hormone are all within normal range. Your heat has passed successfully."

I blink away the haze of sleep, my eyes adjusting to the soft morning light filtering through my blinds. The relief washes over me like a cool shower after three days of burning from the inside out. "Thank you, Two."

Ace stirs beside me, his arm tightening briefly around my waist before he stretches, all languid muscle and uninhibited movement. His eyelids lift, revealing those impossibly blue eyes.

My chest flutters in a way that I can no longer blame on heat hormones.

"Morning," he mumbles, voice still rough with sleep, and pushes himself up on one elbow. But instead of his usual easy smile, his brow furrows, creating a small crease I find myself wanting to smooth away with my thumb.

What's wrong? Did I do something embarrassing last night?

"Two confirms my hormone levels are normal," I report,

defaulting to data as I always do when emotions threaten to complicate matters. "My heat cycle is over."

Ace nods, but the furrow between his brows doesn't disappear. He glances at Two, then back to me, his expression uncharacteristically serious. "Can we talk about something?"

A spike of anxiety shoots through me—a purely psychological response now, not hormonal.

I sit up, pulling the sheet with me in a reflexive gesture of protection. "Of course. What's the matter?"

He sits up too, running a hand through his sleep-mussed hair. The motion releases a fresh wave of his ocean scent, and I inhale deeply before I can stop myself. Even without my heat driving me, his alpha pheromones affect me in ways I find difficult to quantify.

"You said some things during your heat," he begins, no longer looking at me, but instead picking at some invisible dust on the nest. "But there was one thing in particular. You said you wanted me to be your alpha. Like, for real. Not just during your heat cycles."

My breath catches. I remember saying it—of course I do. I remember every desperate word, every plea, every promise I made while the heat consumed me.

But in the clear light of morning, with my biochemistry restored to its normal parameters, I had assumed those declarations would be filed away as heat-induced delirium by both of us.

"I said many things under the influence of elevated hormone levels," I reply carefully, my analytical mind trying to create distance between myself and the vulnerability of that admission.

"I know." Ace's gaze drops to his hands. "That's why I'm asking if you meant it. Or if it was just the heat talking."

One and Three rise to a seated position, flanking Two. They watch us like three guys at the movies, waiting for the drama to unfold.

I feel strangely naked despite the sheet wrapped around me—exposed emotionally in a way I can't hide with linens.

It was just the heat, right?

Yes. Of course. Heat-induced pair bonding is a well-documented biological phenomenon, a temporary insanity designed to ensure reproductive success. Nothing more.

That would be the logical answer.

But when I look up to deliver this perfectly reasonable explanation, I find myself caught in Ace's gaze.

The statistical probability of eyes being that exact shade of blue is vanishingly small. Yet, here they are, looking at me with a mixture of hope and resignation that creates an uncomfortable pressure in my chest.

He is chaos embodied—the antithesis of everything I've built my life around.

And yet. The thought of never looking into those eyes again is more terrifying than letting him into my life...

I take a deep breath, forcing myself to look directly at him despite the discomfort. "When I was in heat, my inhibitions were lowered, and my desire for connection was heightened. That's a biological fact. But..." I pause, searching for the language to describe these emotions that defy categorization. "But I don't think that created feelings that weren't already there. It just... removed the barriers I had constructed around them."

Hope blooms across his face, and I'm struck by how transparently his emotions display themselves—no deception, not even a response molded by unspoken societal norms, just pure, unfiltered Ace. One of the many things I like about him. One of the many reasons he's perfect for me, fulfilling all the needs I didn't even know could be met.

He asks, "So you do want me to be your alpha?"

"Yes," I say, surprised by how easy it is to say. "I do want that."

His smile breaks across his face like sunrise, too bright to look at directly. "For real? Not just when you're in heat and when you need an alpha to help you through it? Not just for research?"

"Yes. For real," I confirm, calmly.

But, suddenly, I feel like I'm stepping off a cliff, the mass of my guts dropping to the ground first. "Though I should note that I have limited experience with conventional relationship paradigms and my interpersonal skills are...suboptimal."

Ace laughs, and it feels like he's peeling my splattered guts off the ground, to hug me and kiss my boo-boos away. "That's the cutest way I've ever heard anyone say, 'I might be bad at dating.'"

Cute? And now I'm the one with a smile spreading across their face.

He moves toward me, one hand gently cradling my face. His thumb traces my cheekbone with a tenderness that makes my breath catch.

"I love you," he says simply. "Not just your scent or your heat or beauty or genius brain—though all those things are pretty awesome. I love YOU. I love all those things and everything else, like how your nose scrunches when you put those scopey things on." He gestures at his head as if he's pulling some magnifying loupes off his forehead and onto his eyes.

Endorphins and oxytocin flood my system in a biochemical response I couldn't suppress if I tried, making his response feel like it hit me with a physical force.

I gulp. *If he really does love everything about me, honesty shouldn't scare him away, right?*

I whisper, looking at his shoulder, "I don't know if I know what love is. I don't know how to tell if I am or am not in love. I don't know what that feels like. I don't know how to measure it or identify it..." Then I meet his face, and he's still smiling, and I smile. "But, I think I love you, too. I'm still working on evaluating all the implications of that statement, so I would appreciate your understanding and patience while I work through that."

He smirks, "So, a different kind of research?"

And I'm hit with another wave of hormones, telling me to run, but not from him, run from myself. *I always pick the wrong fucking thing to say.*

"I didn't—"

"I'm sorry, Cookie, I was just teasing you. I didn't mean to scare you." His laugh is soft against my lips as he pulls me into an embrace. "Everyone has those doubts. We'll figure out what loving each other means to us. That's kind of the whole point."

Really? Everyone finds this confusing? It's not just me?

I allow myself to relax into his arms and rest my head at a perfect angle against his perfect shoulder. I press my nose to his scent gland on his perfect neck and inhale his perfect ocean scent. We fit together with a precision that feels...perfect. The emotions swirling through me are uncategorisable and undefinable; the only word that comes to mind is: *'perfect.'*

It's perfect. Perfectly, unpredictably, perfect.

We embrace like this for a long time, just taking in the full sensory experience of each other.

But Ace breaks the silence. "Will you meet my packmates—Thomas and Forrest?"

I tense involuntarily. "Why?"

He pulls back, looking into my eyes with an earnestness that makes it impossible to look away. "Because they're my family. And because...well, we've talked about finding an omega to complete our pack. Someone who fits with all of us."

Hold on...Evelyn was right?

"And...you think I could be your pack's omega?" I ask.

"I know you could," he says with that maddening certainty he sometimes displays.

I bite my lip. "How? What data do you have to back up that assertion?"

"Well, for one, you're my scent-matched mate."

"WHAT!?"

"Cookie, don't tell me you didn't see my scent—not just smell it—see it, floating around in the air."

"I did."

"You know that means we're scent-matched, right?"

"IT DOES!? I thought it was just because you were super hot

and I was super horny! People don't always see scents when they get like that?"

He laughs. "Nope."

"Oh, wow..." I say, trailing off, feeling like my whole worldview has once again been turned on its head.

"And, I'm already bonded with them. All the smartest scent scientists say that there's a 99% certainty they'll be scent-matches with you, too." His smile is mischievous, suppressing a laugh.

"You're making that up."

"Yeah, but there's gotta be a ton of scientific studies on it that will give you that quant-a-tate-able data you're probably looking for. We can look it up together."

There is. I have a bunch of the studies still saved on my hard drive from when I orchestrated Evelyn's pack formation.

I reply, "Quantitative. And yes, it has been scientifically validated with both quantitative and qualitative studies."

I bite my lip and look down at the nest again.

"But the science isn't what worries you, huh? What is it?"

"What if they don't like me? Being scent-matched, while guaranteeing sexual compatibility, doesn't guarantee compatibility across the other metrics used to determine a successful bonding."

"Why wouldn't they like you?" he asks with an expression so genuinely confused I want to kiss him.

"I'm not exactly..." I gesture vaguely at myself.

"Not exactly what?" Ace challenges gently. "Smart? Beautiful? Fascinating? Kind? Caring? Because you're all those things, Styles."

"Socially compatible," I finish. "I don't do well with people, generally speaking. I say the wrong thing. I don't respond the way they want, usually. I don't know how to determine what they want unless I have my data, my monitors, my bots."

"You do fine with me."

"You're different." I can't quite articulate how or why, but something about Ace reduces my usual discomfort with human interaction.

His smile softens. "I'm just asking you to meet them. The whole scent-match thing, forming a pack, all that, we'll talk about that later—when you're ready. If you meet them and it doesn't feel right, that's fine."

"But...if they don't like me...will you—?"

"You and me will still be us, either way."

I consider this, mentally mapping out the decision tree. Meeting his packmates is a discrete event with a defined beginning and end. It doesn't obligate me to further action, if the interpersonal chemistry proves incompatible. And it matters to Ace—that much is clear from his expression. And, I want to do this for him.

"Okay. If you promise to stand by the conditions you just outlined, I'll meet them."

His face lights up with such joy that I momentarily forget my anxiety. He pulls me close again, pressing his lips to mine in another kiss that I actually enjoy. "Thank you," he murmurs against my mouth.

He pulls back. "I promise—I'm your alpha no matter what. But I know they're going to love you."

Two leans forward slightly, raising his finger in that way he does when he has a question. "Query. If Beth bonds with your pack, will we be decommissioned?"

I look at the three of them and tears well in my eyes. *Will they make me get rid of my bots?*

Ace laughs. "Of course not, brobots! What kind of Prime Alpha would I be if I didn't protect my robo-pack from decommission?"

The three alphabots look relieved, and I'm starting to realize they've learned more than heat management from Ace.

Three crosses his arms. "And will we still be able to participate in heat management? Or will human packmates be sufficient, thus rendering us unnecessary?"

Ace smiles again. "Come on, Three. You've got that fancy spinny cock, and none of you have a refractory period. That's an invaluable skill during an omega's heat."

Three smirks, crossing his arms even tighter. "That is true. We are significantly better at keeping it up than human alphas."

I ask. "You think they'll be okay with the bots? Like, they won't think it's weird or be jealous or whatever?"

Ace's grin remains constant. "Cookie, they're going to love you and your bots. I guarantee it."

I don't share his certainty, but I find myself wanting to believe him.

I suppose I'll find out soon enough.

* * *

Want too know what happens when Styles meets Ace's pack? Read *Love is Knot Efficient.*

Subscribe to my newsletter for updates: https://www.imogenknowed.com/newsletter

A NOTE FROM THE AUTHOR

Thank you so much for taking the time to read *Love is Knot Predictable.*

Please leave a review on Amazon and Goodreads.

If you'd like to keep up with my work, follow me on social media and subscribe to my newsletter:

https://www.instagram.com/imogenknowed

https://www.imogenknowed.com/newsletter

SPECIAL THANKS

I want to thank my husband for his unwavering support while I wrote this book. Without his support, I could not have hyper-focused on it, writing literally every moment of the day that I wasn't working or sleeping.

To my husband:

Thank you for enthusiastically discussing characters and plot with me. Thank you for being okay with the fact that my mind was lost to another world for a while. Thank you for always putting food in front of me when I get so lost in something and forget my own body has needs. Thank you for always being there to help me recover whenever my mind and body explode from the world being too loud, too distracting, and too scratchy. I love you.

ABOUT THE AUTHOR

Imogen Knowed is a queer, AuDHD girly who hyperfocuses on creating fake people in her head. Instead of letting them stay in there, she writes them down for others to meet. She spends her days programming video games and her nights reading and writing smut. When she's not writing smut or making video games, she's hanging out with her family and pets (aka her "pack").

You can follow her on social media:

https://www.instagram.com/imogenknowed
https://www.threads.com/@imogenknowed

www.ingramcontent.com/pod-product-compliance
Lightning Source LLC
La Vergne TN
LVHW010617100826
845148LV00014B/2998